# *Table of Contents*

# Chapter One

## *Up A Tree*

It wasn't that I didn't want to climb. In fact it seemed that it would be fun to be up there with Mother, looking over the wide countryside. And it certainly wasn't that I wished to stay on the ground all alone. It was scary being there all by myself.

But the tree was so tall and so straight. And it seemed such a long, long way up to the lowest branch. The little nails on the ends of my toes looked too weak to dig into the bark and keep my body from falling. If I fell - it was such a long, long way down. And the ground, where I would eventually land with a thump, was so solid and hard. I just knew it would knock the wind right out of me.

I looked up at Mother again and whimpered in fright.

"Come on," she coaxed for the tenth time. "Come on up. You're not safe down there."

I looked up at the tall tree with its branches that seemed to reach the soft, fluffy evening clouds. I felt a lot safer right where I was than where Mother wanted me to be.

I curled up more tightly, tucked my neck in and shut my eyes to block out the sight of the tree and the thought of following Mother up the long, thin trunk.

"Come on," Mother called again.

I opened my eyes and looked at her long enough to respond in a shaky voice, "I can't."

"Of course you can," she said firmly but gently. "All porcupines can climb."

"I can't," I insisted and shut my eyes again.

It became quiet then. I expected to hear Mother urge me further but her words did not come. Rolling into a tight ball, I closed my eyes so firmly that they hurt.

When the silence continued, I became even more afraid. What if Mother was no longer up in the tree? What if she had disappeared and I was on my own? The very thought frightened me so much that my eyes popped wide open again. Stretching out my neck, I tilted my head and peered up the tree trunk. What would I do if Mother was gone?

But there she was. She was no longer up in the high branches feeding contentedly. She was just above my head and moving slowly, surely down the trunk of the tree.

I sighed with relief. I wouldn't need to climb. She was coming back to join me on the ground.

I watched her back all the way down the trunk. By the time her left hind foot reached for solid ground, I was beside her, pushing against her side, anxious to let her know how happy I was to be with her again.

At first she said nothing, just drew me close and held me until my body stopped shaking. Then, still holding me, she talked softly, "Now Pordy," she began. My name is really Pordillia, Por-dil-lia Cammy Porcupine, but Mother calls me Pordy. "Pordy, you have grown too big to stay in the nest in the hollow. You must learn to eat from the trees now. We live up there.''

Mother pointed up the tree among the branches. "It is too dangerous for us on the ground. We can not run as fast as the fox or deer. We can't hide as easily as the rabbits or weasels. We can't dash for a tree as quickly as the squirrels. So we stay up there. Safe. Up in the branches. We are not meant to be ground creatures. We have everything we need up there. Food. Moisture from the rains or dew. A safe place to sleep. Everything.''

She hesitated for a moment and let her words sink in.

Mutely I nodded so Mother would know that I had been listening.

"You understand?" she prodded gently.

I nodded again.

She eased me back from her but I reached out and grasped a handful of her thick, long fur. I didn't want to be deserted again.

But she did not let me curl up against her. She said firmly, "Be careful. Remember the sharp quills.''

I remembered. I had poked into one once and it had stung for hours.

Nodding toward the tall tree, Mother continued, "That is where we are safe. That is where we must go.''

I began to sniffle again. I was absolutely sure that I'd never make it up the tree to that first branch. And if I ever *did* get to the first branch, I vowed I'd never move one step farther. I'd just sit right there and hang on for dear life.

"Now I will go first," Mother was saying. "You watch me carefully and come right behind me. Do just as I do. You will not fall. Porcupines don't fall. The

Creator made us for climbing. It's quite natural and perfectly safe."

Then why did it look so . . . so unnatural and so unsafe to me, I wondered. But I knew better than to answer back to Mother.

She pushed me back away from her and I knew what would happen next. She was going to climb that tree and leave me on the ground again. I couldn't stand the thought. I hated to be alone. I decided to follow her, clinging to her if possible. I reached for another handful of her thick hair and held on tightly as she took her first step toward the tree.

"Now Pordy," she said, turning to look at me, "You can't climb if your hands are full of something else. You'll have to let go of me and use your paws on the tree trunk."

Let go? I couldn't think of it. Mother was my safety. How could I let go and trust my own small paws on the trunk?

"Let go, Pordy," she said again.

I began to shiver again - and I wasn't even off the ground.

"Let go."

I let the handful of Mother's coat slip from my fingers. I wanted to curl up into a ball and close my eyes again. Oh, if only I could go back to the snug nest in the hollow of the tree trunk.

"Now put up the first paw and grab the trunk tightly just like you clutched me," advised Mother.

Still shivering, I reached up one small paw and pressed my claws deeply into the soft bark of the tree.

"Now the other one," said Mother.

I reached up the other paw.

"Now lift yourself slowly."

I lifted, but I was shaking with fright - and I still had my two back paws firmly on the ground.

"Now lift your hind paw and take a hold."

Oh, how I hated to lift that hind paw - but I obeyed, holding my breath as I did so.

Then came the really hard test.

"Now the other hind paw."

Surely not, I thought. If I lift this one, I won't have any foot on the ground at all. What if my paws won't hold? I'll fall right on my back side.

"Lift," said Mother.

I shut my eyes tightly again, a soft cry of fear squeezed out of my shivering body. I prepared for the fall that I was sure would come and slowly, shakily lifted my last paw from the solid ground beneath me. Quickly I stabbed at the tree trunk and dug my claws deeply into the bark. There I clung, shaking, holding my breath, ready for the *thump* as I hit the ground. But nothing happened and the seconds ticked by.

"There," said Mother with a note of satisfaction. "Now raise your front paws one at a time."

Raise them? I was sure that if I tried to move even one paw, the other three would never hold me. Raise them? How could I ever do that without letting go of what I was clinging to so desperately?

"Raise one," prompted Mother.

"I . . . I can't," I trembled. "I . . . I'll fall."

"No, you won't," Mother assured me. "I wouldn't bring you up here if I thought you'd fall. Now, raise one. Just . . . just let your claws relax - open your paw slightly - release your hold - then reach up and take a new hold just a little bit higher.''

It sounded so hard. I was sure that I couldn't do it.

"Easy. Relax - reach - and grab,'' said Mother.

I tried, but it was so hard to relax one paw without letting the rest of me relax, too, and I just knew that if I ever dared to do that, I'd go down with a thump.

At last I managed to find the muscles to the one front paw. Slowly I unclenched my hold. Slowly, ever so slowly, I let the claws pull free of the tree bark. At last my front paw was clear and I tried to concentrate on Mother's next order. Reach, she had said. Reach just a bit higher and grab the tree again. I willed my paw to inch slowly upward but, before I could raise it, panic set in and I shut my eyes and grabbed tightly to the spot that I had just relinquished. I had gained nothing in my attempt. I clung, shivering and whimpering, too scared to move. I was too frightened to even try to get back down to the solid ground I longed for. I could go nowhere and already my legs ached because of my tenseness as I clung desperately to the trunk of the tree.

"Try again,'' said Mother.

"I . . . I can't,'' I cried.

"Yes. Yes, you can. You almost made it that time. Just be a bit bolder. You'll do it.''

Oh, I hated to try. I wanted to just cling to the tree and stay right where I was. But I was already getting tired and there was no safe limb to hold me. I couldn't get back to the ground again. If I stayed where I was, I would become so weary that I would fall for sure. I had to climb. One way or the other. Either up or down and Mother was up.

I finally steeled myself and tried again. This time I made it. I had reached only an inch or so ahead of where my paw had been before. But it was a start. I had made a little progress.

"Now the other one," coaxed Mother.

On up the tree we went. Mother kept pleading and encouraging me as I put one trembling little paw ahead of the other until slowly - very slowly - I was inching my way up the tree. I was getting closer to the branch above my head.

I didn't stop shaking but I did stop whining. It took all my concentration to decide which paw I should move next. I could imagine how dreadful it would be if I'd get mixed up and move the wrong one.

"There," said Mother. Her voice was just above me. I still wouldn't open my eyes. I was too scared. But it was a comfort to know that she was close by.

"There," she said again. "You are almost at the branch. Then you can stop for a rest before going up to feed."

That was both good news and bad news. I was glad that I was almost at the branch and could stop and rest - but I was sorry to hear that Mother expected me to climb still higher. I just wanted to reach that branch and hang on.

# Chapter Two

## *Steady*

I clung to the branch for a long time. My stomach was beginning to growl with hunger. Still I refused to let go of my hold.

Mother was above me feeding contentedly. Every now and then she would look down and encourage me to climb up and share her lunch. But I still refused. The ground was now a long, long way beneath me. I realized how far I had climbed when I dared to look down. The sight made me feel dizzy. What if I were to fall? I shut my eyes and let the dizziness pass.

The round full moon had moved from the east all of the way around to the west. A gentle breeze stirred the tree slightly, giving a strange rocking motion to the limb where I clung. I would have enjoyed it if I had not been so nervous about the possibility of falling.

It didn't seem to bother Mother in the least. On those rare moments when I dared look up to where she fed, I could see her clinging confidently to one tree branch or another. Occasionally I saw her reach out one paw and lean out from the limb where she swayed to grasp a handful of leaves. One time I almost shouted out in fear, afraid that she would fall from her perch.

But Mother seemed quite at home in the branches of

the tree. Even the swaying did not seem to make her dizzy.

As morning began to approach, I was really hungry. I hoped that Mother had finished eating and was ready to climb down to the safety of our overcrowded nest or even the comparative safety of the ground.

Then I remembered. I would need to climb down to join her. I wasn't sure that I could do that. It was hard enough going up the tree and I thought that it would be twice as hard backing down. I decided I'd just stay where I was.

"Aren't you getting hungry?" Mother asked me, coaxing still in her voice.

I nodded, clutching the limb more tightly. Even the little shake of my head made my perch seem more perilous.

"Why don't you come up and eat?"

"I'm . . . I'm fine," I quivered.

Mother seemed to think about my words.

"I guess I'm fine, too," she said at last. "And the sun will soon be up. I guess it's time to take a nap."

A nap seemed like a good idea to me, though I was still worrying about how I would get back down to the ground.

Mother seemed to be quite satisfied where she was situated. I watched as she arranged herself firmly on a limb above me and settled down with a yawn. It looked as though she was planning to take a nap right where she was.

"Mother," I ventured, my voice shaky, "I'm hungry."

"Why don't you eat, dear?" she responded in a

drowsy voice. I was sure that she didn't even open her eyes to look at me.

"I . . . I can't," I answered with a whimper.

"Of course you can, dear," she replied. "You're a porcupine."

She squirmed a bit to find a more comfortable position. I heard her yawn again, then smack her lips slightly as though enjoying the last little taste of food on her tongue.

"But I can't reach the food," I complained.

"Climb, dear," said Mother. She sounded sleepy and content and I knew it would be the last I heard her voice for some time.

I looked up and up. The leaves were above my head. Mother was already breathing gently in sound sleep. I trembled. I dared not look down. I dared not even look up. But one thing I knew for sure. I did need to eat.

Slowly, ever so slowly, one small foot reaching out at a time, I inched my way up toward the leaves that fluttered somewhere above my head.

It was slow, exasperating work, made even more difficult because I was holding my breath. At last I felt something tickling my ear. The wind was waving a twig of leaves just above me. With a few more small advances I would be right up among the leaves. I would be able to feed just as I had seen Mother feed during the night.

Finally I reached a small limb that offered a few leaves within easy reach. The sun was just beginning to push above the eastern horizon. It was time for porcupines to be resting - not eating, but I was so hungry that I had to eat before sleeping.

I ate the few leaves that dangled around me, careful to hang on with all four paws as I plucked them off the branch with my teeth. They tasted so good. I was sorry to run out so quickly. Shifting my weight, I pushed my way farther up the tree to reach a few more. Then lift and reach again. And lift and reach still farther. In my hunger, I almost forgot my fright. Almost, but not quite.

I still trembled each time I pushed myself upward. I still shook whenever I had to stretch to reach another leaf. I still didn't dare to look down toward the ground. I earnestly wished that Mother and I had been born ground creatures.

Mother was still sleeping soundly when I decided that I had eaten enough to pacify my hunger. I didn't know what to do. I hated to awaken her but I had to know what to do next. I had climbed almost halfway up to her but she was still above me, and we were both a long way from the ground.

I cast one quick look downward and saw two rabbits returning to the twisted roots of a fallen tree where they had their home. Their sides bulged and they hopped slowly. I guessed that they had eaten well during the night hours. Again I wished that I had the luxury of hopping a few feet and crawling off to the safety of tangled roots to snuggle down with Mother. Instead, I was treed and Mother slept unconcerned above me.

"Mother," I said in a whisper.

There was no response. She did not even twitch.

"Mother," I tried again a bit louder.

Still no response.

"Mother!" I fairly yelled in my desperation.

"Mother, I need you."

She stirred then and her lips began to smack as though she was remembering how good the leaves had tasted. She didn't even open her eyes, just rearranged her position in the fork of the tree and appeared to be curling up again.

"Mother," I said quickly to catch her before she settled. "Mother!"

Her eyes opened and she looked around as though bewildered. I think that she didn't like the brightness of the morning sun. She seemed confused.

"Mother, I'm down here," I called up to her.

She tipped her head slightly and looked down the tree trunk. When she saw me, a smile flickered across her face.

"Good," she said as though pleased. "You climbed."

"I had to climb to eat," I reminded her.

"Yes," she said, still sounding sleepy. "Good," and she smacked her lips again.

I knew that she was about to doze off again so I quickly continued, "What do I do now?"

Again she looked puzzled.

"What do I do now?" I repeated.

Her eyes lifted to the sun that hung in the morning sky. To our left, two jays squawked and squabbled over the shriveled berries on a nearby berry bush. Mother gave them a brief, disdainful glance and began to close her eyes again. In her distraction she had already forgotten me.

"What do I do?" I called up to her.

She looked down at me with another absent-minded

smile. "You sleep, dear," she told me. "You sleep."

"Where?" I called up. "I can't get down."

I was used to curling up and sleeping in the snug nest that Mother had provided for me.

"Right there, dear," said Mother.

"But I can't," I protested, the fear making my voice quivery. "I can't hang on and sleep at the same time."

Mother roused herself from her sleep with difficulty. I guess she heard the terror in my voice.

"Do you want to go down?" she asked tenderly.

"Yes. Yes," I cried and then quickly amended, "No, no, I can't go down. I don't know how."

"Of course you can, dear," I heard Mother say. I could tell by her voice that she had stirred herself and was moving down toward me.

"Of course you can," she said again. "You just reverse the process. One paw at a time. Relax, reach and grab. Only this time you reach down instead of up."

It sounded easy - but I was just sure that it wouldn't be. I clung there trembling as Mother came down to me. She touched me gently with her nose and then moved around to the other side of the tree so she could pass me on her way down. As soon as she was below me, she came around to my side of the tree again.

"Now I am right here beneath you," she said gently. "Just do as I said. Relax your hold, reach down and grab on again. One paw at a time. Come on now."

The first downward step was the hardest. I was sure that I would fall. It helped to have Mother beneath me. Even then, I was afraid that if I did fall, I would knock her out of the tree and we'd go tumbling down together.

I managed to make that first step. Then another. And

another. I was sweating by the time I heard Mother say with satisfaction, "Here we are now." We had reached our home at the base of the tree.

I was so glad to tumble through the opening and feel something solid beneath my feet again.

Mother eased in behind me. The nest was tight for the two of us. I had a feeling that it was going to be too hot. I wasn't sure if it was because of the warm rays of the sun, or just my nervousness, but I sure felt warm. It would take some time to cool off after my descent from the tree. I curled up on Mother's soft underside because there were no quills there to poke me. Before I could close my eyes, Mother had already fallen asleep. I willed my quivering body to stop shivering and pushed closer to her. It was nice to feel safe again. Smiling to myself, I prepared for a nice, long nap. I hoped that I never had to climb a tree again - never, as long as I lived.

# Chapter Three

## *Learning*

I did not get my wish. That very evening Mother stretched and rolled over after our long sleep together. She opened her eyes and said, "Guess it's time to eat. My stomach is dreadfully empty."

"Where do we eat tonight?" I asked her, still stretching away my own sleepiness.

Mother's eyes popped wide open. "Why, up the tree, of course," she responded.

I felt my own eyes open wide. "Again?" I asked incredulously.

"Of course. That is where we always eat," said Mother and then amended her statement slightly. "At least, almost always. Sometimes, like the rabbits, we find something in a garden. Or some nice juicy plants in the marsh. But I don't think any of them are ready yet."

"Why don't we just wait for them?" I bargained.

"Wait for them? Why, my word, it could be days or weeks before they are ready," laughed Mother.

"But I don't like . . ."

"Nonsense," cut in Mother, "you did just fine once you put your mind to it."

I shuddered to think of the difficult task of climbing

all the way up to the tender leaves - and then back down again. But Mother was already stirring. Her stomach rumbled in gentle pleading to be filled.

"Come along," said Mother as she carefully surveyed the world around us to make sure it was safe to exit our home. For one brief moment I hoped that there was a fox or a bear nearby. Mother had warned me about them and I knew that if one was around she would refuse to leave our nest.

Everything seemed to be quite safe so Mother stepped out of the hole and turned sharply to reach for a paw hold on the trunk. Immediately she began to make her way up the tree toward the leaf dinner above. She did not wait for me to follow but called back over her shoulder, "Come along, dear. Follow close to Mother."

I went. I began to shake again but this time I was determined to keep as close to Mother as I possibly could. I shut my eyes for the first few steps and then opened them to fasten them on Mother's ascending body. She rose slowly and steadily before me and I tried to lift a paw upward each time that I saw her do so. Even then, the distance between us began to widen. I knew that Mother could stretch forward farther than I and the fact that she was getting ahead of me sent panic through my body.

"Mother," I cried after her. "Mother . . . wait. I can't keep up."

She paused and looked down. "You're doing fine, dear," she encouraged me. "Just fine. Much better than last night."

I knew that I was climbing better than the night

before but I was still frightened. I was also puffing. Mother's pace was too fast for me.

She waited until I bumped up against her heel and then she took another step upward. I climbed right along behind her.

When I got to the first limb, I sure could have used a chance to catch my breath but Mother was moving on up to the leaves. I certainly did not wish to be left behind, shaking and hungry as I had been the night before. I continued to climb right below her.

"There's a nice clump," she said, indicating with her nose an overhanging branch covered with dancing leaves.

I looked where she pointed and began to shake again. The leaves were too far from the main trunk of the tree. I shook my head slowly. "They're . . . they're too far away," I panted.

"Then what about these?" asked Mother patiently as she pointed out another swaying branch.

"The branch is too skinny," I answered. Surely it would never hold my weight.

"Well, over here then."

"There are only two leaves. I would just get there and have to move again," I replied.

"Alright," said Mother. "Just keep climbing. There are plenty of good branches just up above your head."

I wanted to protest climbing higher but I bit my tongue. If I wanted to eat, I had to climb. Even I realized that.

At last I did manage to find some leaves in a spot that suited me better. I clung to the tree trunk and plucked them off with my teeth. Mother noticed.

"It is much easier if you reach out with one paw and pick them off," she tried to encourage me.

"I might fall," I insisted.

"You're a porcupine," she reminded me.

I knew that I was a porcupine - and a very nervous one at that. Her remark didn't do one thing to bolster my courage. But gradually, as I ate, my trembling lessened and my self-confidence increased.

It was a pretty night. Overhead the moon shone brightly. Stars twinkled all across the sky and fleecy clouds drifted softly in and out among them. Night noises were all around us. Some I recognized, having heard them before from the safety of our hollow nest. Some were new to me. Whenever I heard one of those I would shiver and wish that I was closer to Mother.

"What was that?" I asked nervously as a strange new sound reached my ears.

"That's a coyote," she responded and went right on feeding.

"Why does he make that awful noise?" I asked.

"He is going on a hunt and wants the other coyotes to know where he is."

"Hunt for what?" I asked next, my nervousness still making my voice quiver.

"For his food," said Mother around a mouthful of leaves.

"Does he eat leaves, too?"

"No."

I waited for just a minute.

"What, then?" I asked.

"Some plants and berries and insects and . . . and small things"

"Like?" My eyes were wide with fright now.

"Well," Mother hesitated. I sensed that she wanted to be honest, yet she did not want to frighten me further. I was already trembling.

"Little things," she said again.

I thought of the little things that I already knew about.

"Rabbits?" I asked her.

"Yes, rabbits - if he can catch them," she answered.

"What else?" I prompted.

"Mice. Gophers. Other little things."

"Porcupines?" I trembled, holding the trunk of the tree with all four paws as tightly as I could.

"They rarely trouble porcupines," said Mother. "They don't like our quills."

I noticed that she hadn't said that they didn't like to dine on porcupine.

"Can they climb a tree?" I asked her nervously.

"No," she answered calmly. "No, they can't climb a tree. They are strictly ground animals."

For the first time I felt thankful to be high up in the tree. I looked way, way down to the ground where night shadows played under the sheltering branches. Something stirred down below in the grasses around the tree trunk. Fear rippled up my spine. I wondered if the coyotes were gathering below me in the hope that a very young porcupine would come tumbling down out of the tree. I held on more tightly, my toes aching with the effort. Off in the distance a coyote cried again.

"I think they have gone off toward the meadow," said Mother around another bite of leaves. "I expect we have heard the last of them for tonight."

It took several more minutes of clinging, holding my breath and straining to listen for any slight movement on the ground beneath us, before I could relax enough to resume my feeding.

At last I felt they had really gone on to do their hunting in other parts of our world. I began to eat again, pushing thoughts of the coyotes from my mind. After several minutes of silent eating, Mother surprised me.

"You remember what to do should you ever be on the ground and a coyote approaches?"

I looked up from my eating, an unchewed leaf sticking out the side of my mouth. I knew I wasn't to talk with my mouth full, so I just nodded my head and hoped that Mother could see the movement by the light of the moon shining above.

"Go through the steps for me," Mother instructed.

I had to chew and swallow quickly. Mother waited patiently.

"Number one - roll in a tight, tight ball," I began.

Mother nodded.

"Number two -" I swallowed the last bit of food in my mouth, "point all my quills."

Mother nodded again.

There was another step but I couldn't think of it. To stall for time, hoping that it would come to mind, I began, "Number three -"

I couldn't remember it. In my mind I went over the steps again. Roll in a ball, raise all my quills, then . . . then . . . what? I still couldn't remember it.

"Your tail?" prompted Mother.

"Oh, yeah, have my tail ready to slap anything that comes near."

"Good," said Mother and I beamed my satisfaction.

But inside I still felt shaky. Was there a chance that I would really meet one of those awful coyotes on the ground? If I did, would I remember the three steps in time? The very thought frightened me. I decided then and there that maybe I'd just stay up in the tree forever and ever.

Then I heard Mother sigh. Or was it a stifled yawn? I lifted my head and noticed that the moon had dropped almost out of sight in the west and the eastern sky was already being washed with a soft, golden glow. Mother had told me that the sun was about to get up from his nap. I knew that it also meant that it was about time for us to take ours. Suddenly I felt very sleepy. My tummy was full and my eyes were heavy. I wondered if I'd even be able to back my way down the tree to the nest in the hollow.

"We'd better go in," said Mother. I knew that she was about to fall asleep right there on her limb.

I remembered that the hollow was right at ground level. I thought of the coyotes and wondered if they were small enough to come into the nest after us. It made me shiver.

"Maybe we could just sleep right here," I said, my voice shaky.

"You want to sleep in the tree?" Mother sounded surprised.

That thought frightened me, too. I wasn't sure which was more scary. Sleeping up high in the tree with the possibility of falling out, or going back down to the ground where I might be discovered by a coyote.

Finally I opted for the tree. "Let's just stay here." I

managed.

"Alright," replied Mother and her voice was already slow with her sleepiness. She yawned. Then she tried to rouse herself so that she could look around us. "There is a nice solid fork just beneath you," she told me. "Why don't you back your way down and settle in there?"

I turned my head far enough to look down the tree trunk. The first thing I saw was the ground, way far beneath me. I shivered again. Then I brought my gaze up the long trunk of the tree to the fork in the branches that Mother had found. It did look rather safe compared to where I was clinging. But I had to maneuver my way back down the trunk. I hated that. It was difficult enough going up, but it was so much worse going down. What if I missed it and went too far? I still kept my eyes closed as I backed down the tree.

Since I was afraid to stay where I was, there seemed to be only one thing to do. Slowly, ever so slowly, I began to ease my way down the trunk, hoping with all of my heart that I would stop at the right time. I had taken only a few steps downward when I heard Mother's soft breathing. Already she was sound asleep. I felt all alone again and I wanted to wake her up so that I wouldn't be on my own.

I managed to check the impulse - at least for a time. Holding my breath, I backed slowly down toward the fork that Mother had selected. It seemed to take forever but I finally reached it. Now I had no idea how to get myself turned around in the right direction to take advantage of the limbs. I wiggled this way and squirmed that way but nothing seemed to turn out right.

Finally I began to whimper. I was afraid I was going to fall with all of my moving this way and that.

"Mother," I called softly.

There was no response and, remembering how loudly I had needed to call her the morning before, I decided not to waste time. "Mother!" I cried loudly.

She jumped and looked wildly around. I am sure that she thought something dreadful must have happened to me.

"What is it?" she asked quickly when she spotted me clinging to the tree trunk.

"How do I do it?" I asked, lowering my voice again.

"Do what?" She sounded deeply puzzled and still quite sleepy.

"How do I get arranged on the limbs for sleeping?" I was a bit impatient that she didn't realize exactly what my problem was.

"Just move," she responded simply.

"Move how?" I whined.

"Move one paw at a time until you have yourself where you want to be," she explained. I knew that she was trying hard to be patient. I could hear it in her voice.

"But I can't. I tried," I complained.

"Try some more," she said encouragingly, and she rolled herself a little tighter in the fork that she occupied. I knew that she was anxious to get back to sleep again.

"I can't," I whined.

"You can. Just one paw at a time. Slowly work your way to just the right position."

There seemed nothing else to do but to keep on

trying. I released one paw and placed it closer to where I wanted to be. Then I moved one hind paw and eased myself forward a little and to the left.

"That's right," said Mother sleepily as she shuffled her weight on the limb and let her eyes close again. I knew that she was already sleeping - but I was making progress. If I just kept moving little by little, I would soon be where I needed to be.

Slowly I moved myself into the fork close to the trunk of the tree. But I did not release my hold on the branches beneath me. I was afraid that I would roll in my sleep and go tumbling to my death. It was hard to hold firmly and yet relax enough to get some sleep. Each time that I started to doze off, I would jerk awake again and cling desperately to my branch. Then I would press my body into the fork so tightly that I wondered if I'd ever be able to free myself again.

At last I must have dropped off to sleep for the next thing I knew Mother was stirring above me and the day was almost spent again.

## Chapter Four

# *A Journey*

"I think that we should move," said Mother a few nights later, catching me by complete surprise. I was just getting used to feeding in the high limbs of our tree.

"Move where?" I asked, forgetting to wait until I had emptied my mouth of some tasty green leaves.

"I'm not sure," said Mother. "We'll know when we get there."

It sounded risky to me.

"How do we move?" I asked hesitantly. I had seen the squirrels leap from one tree to another. I certainly hoped that Mother wouldn't ask me to try that. The closest tree seemed a long way off.

"We just climb down and walk to where we want to go," she answered me, very unconcerned.

I thought about the coyotes. I thought about foxes. I even thought about bears - though I had never seen one.

"What . . . what about the . . . the . . . the bad animals?" I stuttered.

"What bad animals?" asked Mother. Then she continued, "There are no bad animals, only hungry animals."

"Well, what about the . . . the hungry coyotes and the foxes and . . ."

"We'll watch out for them," said Mother.

"Why don't we just stay here and . . ."

"There isn't much left to eat in this tree and I am a little tired of this menu. I'd like something different for a change."

I really wasn't tired of what we had been dining on for the last week. But I had no idea what else was available. Still, I hated the thought of lowering myself onto the ground.

Mother was already backing slowly down the tree trunk. She had definitely made up her mind. I felt a shiver of fear run up my spine. I tried hard to stifle it before it came out in a whimper. "Can't we stay here?" I pleaded one more time.

"Come on, Pordy," said Mother. "You'll like what I find for us. You'll see."

Now that she had made up her mind, Mother seemed to be eager to start. I knew there was no use arguing further. If I didn't want to be left behind, I had to get down the long trunk of that tree.

Slowly, paw by paw, I made my way to the bottom of the tree. Before I reached the ground I stopped and took a look around to see if I could spot any coyotes. The only problem was, I had never seen a coyote. I wondered if they jumped like the squirrels or hopped like the rabbits. Maybe they flew like the owl. But no, that didn't seem right. If they were able to fly and liked to dine on porcupine, then they would have been right up that tree to get us. I decided that they must not be able to fly.

Mother had reached the ground and was ambling off toward the direction of the rising moon. I took a quick breath, held it and landed on the ground with a plop. Picking myself up as quickly as I could, I hurried off after her.

We walked for a long time. Mother had told me that we could not move as quickly as the deer or the foxes. As I scrambled along behind Mother, trying desperately to keep up with her, it seemed to me that we were traveling at a terrible clip.

"Where are we going?" I finally managed to say between puffs.

"To the orchards," replied Mother.

"What are orchards?" I panted.

"More trees," said Mother.

I looked around me. We were traveling through trees and had been ever since we left our home. I wondered why Mother felt that she had to go farther to find trees.

"These are trees," I told Mother indicating with my nose the growth all around us.

"Not orchard trees," said Mother.

"What are orchard trees?" I was panting so hard that I could hardly get the words out.

"You'll see," said Mother. She was not panting at all. In fact, she seemed to be moving slowly as she waddled through the tiny shrubs and tall grasses at the base of the large trees.

"How much farther?" I puffed. I was still spending a lot of time looking over my shoulders, first this way, then that. I was thinking about the coyotes and foxes and bears and hoping that they weren't too hungry, nor too close.

"A ways," said Mother casually.

"How much is a ways?" I was close to whimpering.

Mother stopped and I almost bumped into her. I was glad that her quills were relaxed. She turned to me and nudged me gently with her nose.

"It's okay, Pordy," she tried to soothe me. "If I thought there was danger I would not take you to the orchard."

"It's not the orchard I'm afraid of," I said, my voice trembling.

"What, then?" asked Mother.

"The . . . the coyotes," I managed, looking over my shoulder with a shiver.

"I haven't heard one coyote all evening," said Mother confidently.

I was just beginning to feel good about that when Mother turned and started walking. She had taken only a few steps when she said something that shook my confidence again.

"If we should meet one, just remember the three rules."

I stopped right in the middle of a step and my whole body trembled. Mother must have sensed my fright for she stopped again and turned to look at me.

"What's the matter, Pordy?" she called back to me.

"I'm . . . I'm scared," I cried. "I . . . I don't even know what a coyote looks like. How . . . how will I know if . . ."

"If *any* large animal comes near, follow the three steps," said Mother. "Whether it's a coyote or not."

"There . . . there are more big animals?" I stammered.

Mother took a few steps back to where I shook in my tracks. "Pordy," she said, and I could tell she was trying hard to be patient again. "You must get over being so frightened of everything. We'll be all right."

"But . . . you said they can run faster . . ."

"They can."

"And . . . and you said they have sharp teeth."

"They do."

"And you said they . . . they get . . . get hungry."

"Yes, they do."

I couldn't bear my next thought without shaking all over. "And you said they . . . they like porcupine."

Mother still seemed unruffled. "They do," she answered me honestly. "But the Creator has not left us defenseless. Don't forget that."

"But we can't run . . ."

Mother interrupted before I could go through the list of things that we could not do.

"I know we can't run fast, or dash up a tree, or fly off, or scamper into a burrow, or dive into the water or any of those things. But we do have our quills." Mother seemed quite confident that our quills would protect us. I still wasn't sure. I just sat right there and shivered.

"Now come, Pordy," she urged me. "We will get to the orchard too late to even have time to eat."

I was hungry. We had not fed on the leaves from the branches long enough to appease my growing appetite. I was still very hungry and the walk had certainly not helped my growling stomach.

I fell into step behind Mother and we continued to waddle our way toward the orchard. But it took so long. I was sure that Mother must have forgotten the way and got us lost in the endless acres of trees.

As I was about to protest by sitting down stubbornly

and refusing to take another step, Mother looked back over her shoulder and said with satisfaction, "Here we are."

All I could see was a whole lot of wire.

"We need to get through the fence," Mother explained and then I heard her talking to herself. "Now let's see. Where was that opening? Over here? No, I think over there."

I followed her, having no idea what she was looking for or what she would do when she found it.

"Oh, my," I heard her say. "They have gone and boarded it up. What a shame. Now we'll need to find another way."

I scrambled along behind her and we went this way and that way along the wire. It seemed totally hopeless to me but Mother wouldn't give up.

"There's got to be a way," I heard her murmur. I kept hoping that she'd give up and head for home again. I was hungry and scared and tired from walking.

"Ah, here we are," I heard her say with satisfaction. Before I knew what had happened, she disappeared from my sight.

"Mother," I called nervously. "Mother, where are you? Where'd you go?"

"Sh-h-h, Pordy," her voice came back to me. "We don't want to waken the farm dogs."

"Dogs? What are dogs?" I asked, feeling even more scared.

"They . . . they're rather like coyotes." Mother informed me in a whisper.

That really made me nervous. It seemed that I had possible danger all around me and I couldn't find

Mother.

"This way," I heard her say. "Right over here. Just crawl through the high grass and under the fence. Something has made a nice tunnel for us."

"Probably a coyote," I muttered glumly. "And the minute I stick my nose under the fence, he'll grab me."

But Mother was now on the other side of the wire and I knew that I had to get to her. Even though it made me dreadfully nervous, I followed her orders. It was dark and scary as I went through the little tunnel on my stomach. I was glad when I poked my nose up on the other side and saw Mother waiting for me.

"Now let's hurry," she coaxed. "We don't have much time left."

I followed Mother. The orchard trees were not as tall as the trees we had left in the forest. Mother seemed awfully anxious to climb one. We hadn't gone far when she picked one out and started up.

The trunk was not as large as the tree I was used to climbing and I found it hard to climb. Mother was already far ahead of me.

"Come on," she called back to me softly and I recalled the dogs she had mentioned.

Before I had settled myself and had time to ask what we were looking for, I heard Mother speak again. "What a shame," she said. "The apples haven't set yet."

"Haven't what?" I asked a bit too loudly for she hushed me again.

"Haven't set," she said again. "They are scarcely more than blossoms. What a shame. All that way for nothing." She sighed and then said with resignation,

"Well, we'd better get back. The night is going fast."

I felt scared, dreadfully hungry and a little upset. Had we come all that way, wasted a night's feeding time, and now would need to travel all the way home again on an empty stomach? I felt like crying.

Mother was lowering herself to the ground.

"I did notice one thing," she said with some satisfaction. "There is a new board over at the hot beds." She seemed really pleased about it.

"A board?" I asked lamely.

"You'll love it," she said and she was almost smacking her lips. "It takes a bit of work but it has the most tasty salt tucked inside. Let's go get some before we travel home. I haven't had a good snack of salt for months."

Mother led the way through the orchard trees. My curiosity was aroused. I could hardly wait to discover what had Mother so excited.

"What's salt?" I asked in a whisper as we walked, but she seemed to not even hear me. She was in a great hurry to reach the treat that lay ahead.

## Chapter Five

## *Treat or Threat*

Mother reached a strange box-like something built up from the ground and stopped short. I saw her touch it with her nose, scramble a little farther, lift her body up onto it and begin to run her nose over it again.

"Salt," she said with satisfaction.

"Where?" I asked innocently.

"In here," she told me. "Right inside this board."

"Why is it in there?" I asked her.

"That's just the way it grows," she answered me.

"How do we get it out?"

"We have to chew it out."

"Chew it out? That'll take forever. What if the . . . the dogs come?"

"We'll work quietly," said Mother. "Come on. Up with you."

Nervously I hoisted myself up beside Mother. "Now watch me," she whispered, "and just do as I do." She began to chew on one corner of the board that built the frame.

It looked rather silly to me but I decided to obey Mother. The board didn't taste good at all.

"Just spit it out," Mother advised me.

It seemed foolish to chew and spit, but I did.

It wasn't long until I heard Mother say, "Um-m-m-m." I lifted my head to look at her. What had she found that I hadn't?

"Um-m-m-m," she said again, smacking her lips.

"What is it?" I couldn't help but ask.

"Salt," said Mother. "Haven't you reached any yet?"

"Guess not," I replied. I had found nothing at all to say, "Um-m-m" about.

"Here, have a lick of mine," offered Mother.

I moved over and pushed my nose to where she had been working on the board. I was still feeling doubtful but, with one lick of my small tongue, I quickly changed my mind.

"Um-m-m-m," I said as I smacked. I licked again. "Um-m-m-m." I was reluctant to give Mother back her spot. I guess she realized it for she shifted over to where I had been gnawing and said as she moved away, "You go ahead and eat there. I'll work on this spot that you got started."

It was fine with me. I just continued gnawing and licking my lips and murmuring soft um-m-m-m's to myself. I had quite forgotten how scared I had been feeling. I had forgotten how tired my legs were from walking. I had even forgotten that I was hungry. I just kept chewing and licking. Mother worked steadily beside me, licking up salt for herself.

Much too soon she stopped. "That's enough for to-night," she said and I hungrily wanted to protest.

"We'll come back tomorrow," she said to encourage me to quit. I still ran my tongue over the chewed board.

"We must go," she prompted again. "The sun will soon be up."

I hated to leave but Mother was backing off the little platform and I didn't want to be left behind. I took one last lick and also backed over the side of the strange construction.

We made our way through the tunnel under the wire fence and started back through the trees. Soon I began to feel thirsty. Mother was ahead of me working her way quickly through the tall grass. I knew that she was anxious to reach safety and to sleep. But I just couldn't keep scurrying after her.

"I'm thirsty," I called out to her.

She looked over her shoulder. "I know," she answered. "I'm thirsty, too."

She kept right on walking. I felt more thirsty with each step. The morning sun was peeking over the eastern horizon and touching the dancing leaves above our heads with shimmering golden light. I longed to stop and rest. I longed for a drink. Mother kept right on walking.

"It's such a long way," I complained.

"We won't go all the way back to our old tree," said Mother.

Her words made me feel good and bad at the same time. I was glad that we wouldn't need to retrace our steps all the way back but I was scared at the thought of not being in my own familiar nest.

"Where will we live?" I asked anxiously.

"We'll pick another tree. One that suits us," replied Mother. "I think I'd like a fir this time. Give us a little change of diet."

I wasn't sure what a fir was but if the change to our diet was as nice as the salt treat had been, I was sure that I would like it. I was still hungry in spite of the fact that our night of feeding seemed to be over.

"I'm thirsty," I said again.

"I know," replied Mother. "There is a stream up ahead."

I had never seen a stream but I looked forward to it now if it would help my thirst.

"What's a stream?" I asked Mother. "Is it a kind of tree?"

"No," said Mother. "Not a tree. It's made of water. Like the dew or the raindrops only there are lots and lots of them all together."

It sounded wonderful.

"Why haven't we gone to the stream before?" I asked as I hurried along after Mother. I could remember being thirsty on other occasions - though not as thirsty as I was feeling now - and Mother had never taken me to the stream before.

"We don't go there much because too many other animals go there," Mother told me.

I stopped dead still. "Like coyotes?" I asked, my eyes opening wide.

"Coyotes go there," replied Mother but she didn't stop walking.

"Bears?" I called after her, still not willing to move forward.

"Bears go there," said Mother.

I stood, frozen, afraid to go forward but even more afraid to be left alone. Mother was far enough ahead of me now that I feared I might lose her in the tall grasses.

"Mother! Wait!" I called loudly and started walking again. My short legs made my whole body wobble with my hurried effort.

Mother stopped and waited for me to catch up.

"I don't want to see the coyotes," I said in panic.

"We need water," Mother reminded me.

"But . . ."

"Now dear," said Mother, "don't you worry. You do remember the three rules, don't you?"

"Yes," I trembled. I did remember the rules. At least I thought I would remember, but if they were put to the real test, I wasn't sure if they would actually work.

"Just curl, point your quills, and be ready with your tail," said Mother and she didn't even slow her walk.

It sounded so easy. But I still doubted if it would really work like it was supposed to.

Suddenly Mother stopped and I bumped up against her hind leg. "There," she said with satisfaction. "I can smell the water now."

I lifted my nose and wiggled it back and forth. I could smell many things in the forest. I wasn't sure what they all were. I sniffed again.

"Right over here," said Mother and she led me forward again.

She walked more slowly now. Each step she took was guarded and deliberate. Occasionally she would stop and sniff the air again. I wondered if she was confused about the water, or if she was checking for something else.

I could see sunlight ahead on the trail. It meant that somewhere up ahead of us was a clearing in the trees.

Mother had told me about clearings and how the bright sun could be so dazzling that one had to squint one's eyes.

"The stream is right through there," said Mother.

I could detect the smell of water then. I was so thirsty. I wanted to burst right out into the bright morning and thrust my nose into wherever the stream was and drink and drink. But Mother held me back.

"Sh-h-h," she said. "We need to approach cautiously. We must check to see which other animals might be ahead of us."

It was hard to stay back but Mother insisted that she be allowed to approach the stream first. Slowly she advanced, stopping often to check the morning breeze for any scents that might be carried in the wind.

She was almost into the sunlight before she turned and nodded for me. "We seem to be alone," she told me and I knew that was my permission to creep ahead and join her.

The sunlight was bright. So bright that I could hardly keep my eyes open as I walked the short distance to the stream. My eyes watered and wanted to go shut, but I kept fighting the feeling and tried hard to keep them open. Even so, I felt blinded and was glad that Mother was ahead of me leading the way.

At last we reached the edge of the stream and I was able to push my nose into its cool water and drink and drink. My, I was thirsty.

When I finally stopped and caught my breath, I looked up at Mother. She had lifted her head, too, and water was still dripping from her chin. She stuck out a red tongue and licked at the drops on her lips and chin hair.

"Why was I so thirsty?" I panted. I hadn't even stopped for breath while I drank.

"The salt," Mother reminded me. "Salt is good but it also makes you thirsty."

I thought it was very strange but I didn't argue with Mother. I thrust my nose into the water for another long drink.

When I lifted my head again, Mother was moving back from the stream. Her sides seemed to bulge with all of the water that she had enjoyed. I wanted to giggle. Then I looked down at my own sides. They were just as round and plump. For one moment I did giggle and then I started to worry. Would I be able to climb to safety in a tree with so much water in my tummy?

"Come on," said Mother. "It is past our bedtime. We must get up into a tree."

"I don't know if I can climb," I fretted.

Mother looked at me and then down at herself.

" We did drink a bit too much," she admitted. "Perhaps we can find a hollow in a log or stump.

Mother managed to find a place where we could sleep in safety without climbing. I was thankful but I was frightened, too. We weren't very far away from the stream. If other animals came there frequently, what was to stop them from discovering us? Two bulging porcupines, tucked as far as they could fit among the roots of a tall pine tree. Two porcupines that should have been safely tucked up somewhere in its branches.

"I hope a coyote doesn't come," I whimpered and Mother drew me a little closer.

"We're fine," she tried to assure me.

I glanced over her back which was turned to the opening in the tree roots.

"If one should come snooping around, I'll just raise my quills," she told me. "I don't think he'll want to poke his nose into that."

I hoped that Mother was right but I still would have felt much more comfortable back in my own nest. I would have felt even more comfortable up in the branches of a tree.

"We must get some sleep," Mother told me. "The sun is already climbing high in the sky."

I tried to nod my head but I was curled up too close to Mother. Closing my eyes, I licked my lips and tasted a grain of salt stuck to my chin hair.

I grinned to myself. The salt had sure tasted good.

I knew that Mother was very sleepy but I had to know something.

"Mother?" I whispered.

There was no answer.

"Mother?" I said louder, tugging gently on the front paw that lay across me. She stirred slightly.

"Mother? Mother can we go eat some more salt when the moon comes up again?"

One eye opened just a fraction. She smacked her lips as though remembering the fine taste of our last feeding. "We'll see," she said and closed her eye again.

It was hard to get comfortable with my sides bulging so I squirmed a bit. The soft needles of the pine provided a cushion and I wriggled again and then settled in. I surely did hope that we'd be able to go back to the orchard for another salt feed. I closed my sleepy eyes. Right now the one thing I needed more than

52

anything else was a good day's sleep.

## Chapter Six

## *Forest Creatures*

I knew that I was growing. As I looked at Mother and then at myself, I could tell that I was no longer so small in comparison. Besides, Mother kept making pleased little comments like, "Look at you, Pordy! You're growing like a weed." Or, "My, My! You're a big girl for your age." Or, "You'll soon catch your mother."

Mother seemed pleased that I was growing. I was pleased, too, but I still felt nervous and dreadfully in need of having Mother close beside me.

However, one thing was changing. I didn't know how to express it but I could sense it. I was lonely. Even with Mother beside me, I still felt lonely. I would sit and watch the other forest creatures as they traveled by twos or threes and think how nice it must be to have other family members. I would listen to excited young animals call across the glade to friends and think how enjoyable it would be to really know someone by name.

As I listened carefully, gradually I put a few names and young creatures together by association. I never did get to meet the individuals. But when I would hear a young squirrel call out, "Hi, Jugsy," I'd study the animal addressed carefully so that I would remember who he was in the future.

How I wished that I could get to know some of the forest young - but I just knew that day would never come. I was much too shy to make their acquaintance and, besides, I just knew that none of them would ever want me for a friend.

Still, it was hard to hide my desire to be a part of the forest play. Maybe Mother knew how I felt for I often noticed her eyes on me as I longingly watched the activity beneath our tree.

Often the games were played in the meadow or the glade just beyond our preferred cluster of trees. One day, hearing a good deal of excitement beneath our tree, I woke up from my daytime nap and looked down to see a whole cluster of young creatures.

"Mother! Look!" My voice trembled with excitement. They were gathering for one of their games right at the foot of our tree. I had never been able to see their playful exchange so close before and I was absolutely mesmerized by it.

The rabbit family members were the most vocal. Jugsy excitedly barked out orders as to how the game should be played. Tugsy hopped back and forth exclaiming, "That's right. That's right," after everything that his brother said. Little Topsy Rabbit just grinned and nodded her head vigorously.

The squirrel triplets seemed impatient to get the game under way. They ran around, up and down the trunk of the big pine tree, chattering until the evening air was filled with their voices.

Freddie, the skunk, waited quietly, a tiny smile playing about the corners of his mouth.

In the limbs above his head, the jays squawked and

clamored, passing on Jugsy's instructions with added words of their own, while the sparrows darted here and there as though all of their wings were attached to the same string. When one lit, they all lit. When one lifted, they all lifted. Any small stirring was enough to make the nervous little birds take flight. The robins sat demurely, seeming neither impatient nor flighty.

I could hardly wait for the game to begin.

"Where's Spoof?" asked Jugsy, with a hint of irritation. "He said he'd be here."

I didn't know Spoof. I had never heard his name before. Was he another rabbit? A squirrel? Or perhaps another skunk?

"He's always late. You know that," Tugsy was saying.

"He'd better hurry or we'll play without him," said one of the squirrels. "Mother won't let us stay out much later."

The day was just ending and the moon was beginning to peek over the eastern horizon. It was the best part of the whole day. I couldn't imagine why the squirrels' mother would be sending them off to bed. Mother had told me that some animals slept at night and did their feeding and other chores by daylight. It seemed terribly backward to me but Mother said that each animal had the right to do things their own way.

"I say we start," said the biggest squirrel. "If he comes, he can join us."

There was a loud chorus of agreement and Jugsy lifted his paw for silence. "Our first game is Tag," he said. "You remember the rules. No going beyond the set boundaries. You can't sit up on the branches.

Everyone has to take a turn being sentry and if he spots
a fox or a coyote, he must be sure to warn everyone -
loudly.''

I had been really excited about the game until he
mentioned the fox and coyote. Then I started to shiver.
The game seemed a bit risky. I was glad that I was
safely up in the branches of the tree.

The game started with a flutter of wings, scamper of
paws and loud excited voices. In spite of my fear of the
foxes, I found myself enjoying all of the commotion.

Mother fed contentedly. I didn't think that she was
aware of what was going on until she turned and spoke
softly to me, ''Why don't you go down and join them,
dear?''

Her words surprised me. They were having so much
fun. I was sure that they wouldn't want me to join them.

I hung my head and felt my cheeks coloring with
embarrassment.

''They wouldn't want me,'' I stammered.

''Did they say they didn't want you?'' asked Mother.

''No-o-o,'' I admitted.

''Then how do you know?''

''Well, I . . . they . . . they . . .''

''Why don't you ask them? Would you like me to ask
for you?''

''Oh no,'' I hastily told Mother, afraid for one awful
moment that she would embarrass me in front of all the
young animals. ''I . . . I don't want to play,'' I hurried
on.

Mother looked at me with questions in her eyes.

''I don't want to play,'' I insisted again.

I just knew that they'd never want to play a game

with me. I just knew. If Mother were to ask them and they had to say it right out loud, why, I'd just be humiliated to death.

Just then a roar went up from below.

"Here's Spoof."

"Hi-ya, Spoof."

"We thought you'd never get here."

"We've already started."

"We thought you had forgotten."

I looked down at the animal I had never seen before.

"Who's that?" I asked Mother before I could check my tongue.

She glanced down briefly, her jaw still working on the rich bark she was chewing. "That's a woodchuck," she said. "Don't know which one."

"Spoof," I informed her. "His name is Spoof."

She nodded and went right on eating.

"Why haven't I seen him before?" I continued.

"They hibernate late," said Mother. "There isn't much for them to eat until things start to grow well." She took another bite. "But they should have been up long before now," she continued. "They're not too active, really."

Mother shared the information in a very matter-of-fact fashion. She was not criticizing the woodchuck family.

He seemed so different from the darting squirrels or quick-hopping bunnies. He didn't move about as quickly as the young skunks. In fact his movements were rather slow and deliberate. Something like my own. But the gang down below seemed genuinely glad to see him. I couldn't understand it.

"You can take my turn, if you like," one of the squirrel triplets was calling.

"The boundaries are the same as last time," interjected Jugsy.

"It's Jimmy Jay's turn to be sentry," Tugsy called out.

The new arrival just stood and grinned, nodding his head to let everyone know that he was receiving all of the information.

"We can play only a few more minutes and then Mother says we have to go to bed," stated one of the squirrels.

"Then we'd better get playing," said the newcomer. The others all hooted agreement and the game went on. I couldn't help but watch. The game got more exciting after the arrival of Spoof. I wondered why. He sure wasn't much to look at. And he couldn't hop like the bunnies or dart like the squirrels. He wasn't as noisy as some of the other players, either. But it was true that they seemed to have more fun after he joined the game. It really puzzled me. Why were they so excited about his joining them - and why didn't they want me?

The game ended as soon as Mrs. Squirrel called to the triplets. I heard her shrill voice ring out over the chatter of the players. "Millicent! Alphonso! Rodney! Time for bed."

The three squirrels looked as if they wanted to coax their mother to stay out a bit longer, but not a one of them voiced the request. Instead they shrugged their shoulders and turned reluctantly toward the tree that housed their nest.

"We'll play again tomorrow night," Spoof called

after them.

They turned long enough to call their agreement and then they were gone.

"We've got to go, too," said the sparrows, all lifting together and heading off toward the thicket of willows.

"Good night. See ya," called the jays noisily, and they, too, left the gathering. The robins shrugged and flew toward the orchard.

The others soon began to disband as well. I knew that the game was over for the night. I hated to see them all leave but I was getting really hungry. Mother had been feeding steadily for an hour or so but I had been much too interested in the game to pay attention to my hunger. As the last shadow disappeared in the under-growth, I sighed deeply and began to eat.

I envied them more than I would have admitted. They'd had so much fun. It would be absolutely won-derful to have so many friends, I thought. And to have such good times together. Me - I would be happy if I had just one friend of my very own. Even if I couldn't run and play in the games. Just to have a friend, a real friend, would be so special.

But I didn't have a friend. I was sure that the other forest creatures were not interested in making friends with a porcupine. I wasn't pretty and I was slow and I was rather hard to get acquainted with, I supposed. At least, I had noticed that Mother wasn't greeted in too friendly a fashion whenever we met forest creatures as we traveled about.

It was easy for the little animals in our woods to make friends with one another. They were much alike. But I knew that I was different. I wasn't sure just what the difference was, but I knew deep down within me that there was a difference. And I was sure that, because of the difference, I would never, ever have a real friend of my own.

# Chapter Seven

## *The Orchard*

"Mother, can we go back to the orchard?" I asked a few nights later.

The evening games of the other forest young had ended some time earlier. Even the rabbits had gone home to bed. The moon was already in the western sky and it wouldn't be too long until the sun would again make its appearance.

Then a new idea hit me. If I could find some way to get to the salt - and if I could share the news with the other young creatures of the forest - then maybe, just maybe, they would accept me as a friend.

The thought nearly took my breath away. I was sure that they would all love the salt every bit as much as Mother and I did. They would be so pleased that I had found it for them.

I didn't dare talk to Mother about my idea. I wasn't sure if she would think it wise to share our salt with all of the other animals. Surely, if it meant that I could win friends, it would be worth it.

I tucked the idea away and moved closer to Mother. I still wasn't sure how to go about my little plan, but I knew that I would work on it and try to find some way. There had to be a way. There just had to.

With further thought, I realized that perhaps the best plan would be to keep the source of the salt a secret for Mother's sake. I could find some way to carry back a piece of the plywood so the other creatures could chew out their own salt. They would love it. I smiled to myself.

I was getting awfully tired of eating the same thing night after night. I had thought the bark had quite a nice distinct flavor when Mother first introduced me to it. Now I was tired of it.

Mother lifted her head and looked at me. Then she tilted her head to look up at the sky.

"It's a little late to be traveling so far tonight," she told me.

"Aw, please," I coaxed.

"It's a long walk to the orchard," continued Mother.

"We can hurry," I responded.

Mother glanced at my short legs. "We can't hurry, Pordy," she said primly. "You know that."

"But we can," I argued further. "We won't stop to eat or rest or anything."

Perhaps Mother began to think about the good things that the orchard might hold. At any rate, I felt that I was making some headway in my coaxing. She didn't seem quite as determined to get to bed at the proper time.

"Well . . ." she began and I decided to press further.

"We won't need to come all the way back here. We can spend the day in one of the orchard trees."

"No," said Mother and she sounded quite firm about it. "It wouldn't be wise for us to stay in the orchard over the day."

"Why?" I prodded.

"It's too busy there. The dogs run in and out. The people travel back and forth. Someone might spot us."

"But we'd stay up in the tree," I insisted.

"Even trees aren't safe with . . ." Mother stopped. I wasn't sure what she was thinking for she did not finish her thought.

"Maybe we'd have time to get back to the trees by the river before morning," she mused. Was she speaking to me or talking to herself?

"Then we can go?" I pressed her.

"If we hurry," she answered and began to climb down the tree.

It was farther to the orchard than I remembered. I thought we'd never get there.

"Some of the apples may be forming by now," Mother thought out loud as we traveled. I knew that the thought pleased her.

I was busy thinking about the fine-tasting salt that we had coaxed from the plywood. It had been a long time since I had tasted anything quite as good as that.

"Remember," warned Mother, "keep a careful eye out for the dogs."

I nodded. The thought of the dogs made me shiver but we had been in the orchard before and no dogs had bothered us. I figured that we ought to be able to sneak in again.

"I wonder if we'll have trouble with the fence," said Mother. "It seems that someone is always messing with the fence. Changing it this way and adding on that. Don't know how a body is to ever find their way around. Wish they'd just leave it be. We just get the way in all figured out and someone goes and changes things again. You'd think they didn't want to have a way to get in to the orchard.''

I nodded again, remembering the awkward fence from the time before. It had taken Mother some time to find the tunnel that went under it.

"We'll just use the tunnel again," I prompted Mother.

"If someone hasn't filled it with rocks or pounded on boards," said Mother and she sounded quite annoyed.

By the time we reached the fence it was getting quite late. I could see Mother cast a nervous glance toward the eastern sky.

"I'm afraid we have very little time to feed before morning is due," she said. "Especially if it takes us long to find a way in."

I wanted to suggest that Mother look in one direction and I'd take the other but I was too scared to go by myself. I followed right at Mother's heels, hoping that she'd be quick to discover a way into the orchard. But it seemed to take us a long time to find a small opening under the fence. Mother had to work hard to enlarge the hole enough for us to squeeze through. By the time we entered the orchard, she was puffing from the hard work of digging.

"Come this way," she called softly to me and made her way straight toward the apple trees.

I followed though my real interest lay in the plywood structure that I knew was against the far fence.

I watched Mother climb an apple tree and begin to sniff her way along the branches. I decided that I wouldn't even bother going up unless there was something worth going for.

"Are they ready?" I called up to Mother.

She sounded terribly disappointed. "They are still awfully small," she called back down. I was relieved to hear it. I didn't know how apples tasted but I was sure that they couldn't compare with the salt in the plywood.

"Then why don't we go get some salt?" I said to Mother as though the idea had just hit me.

"Salt? Yes, some salt would be nice now that we are here."

I had to stand and wait while Mother backed her way slowly down the tree trunk. She took her time turning around once her four paws had touched the ground. Her nose wiggled and her whiskers twitched. I could hardly wait for her to begin moving toward the plywood frame.

When we reached the spot, I was terribly disappointed. All around the plywood someone had placed a thick wire mesh. We couldn't crawl through it, we couldn't climb over it and there seemed no way to wriggle under it. I felt like crying.

"How are we ever going to reach it?" I asked Mother.

"We'll have to find a way to dig under the wire," she said.

My hope was renewed. "Can we?" I asked excitedly.

"Well, I'm sure we'll be able to find some way - but not now. It's already too late. We'll have to leave before the dogs start stirring. We'll come back tonight."

I wanted to argue but the thought of the dogs had me looking over my shoulder, studying the shadows. I was disappointed. I had been so hungry for some of the delicious salt.

"Well, come now," said Mother. "We must be out of here before the sun starts climbing," and she led the way back toward the hole under the fence.

I followed but I didn't walk very fast. It was so disappointing to have to leave without one little taste of salt.

We returned to the orchard that very night. I could hardly wait to try again. In fact, Mother seemed very anxious also. I think that she must have been thinking about the salt all day long as she slept for often I would hear her lips smacking in her sleep and I supposed that she was thinking of how good the salt would taste again.

As soon as the sun went to bed and the moon began to rise, we stirred ourselves. Mother seemed just as eager as I was.

"It might take us a while to find our way in," she warned me, "so I guess we should get going"

I agreed. I was more than anxious.

We plodded toward the orchard. This time Mother went right to the hole under the fence.

We were foiled again. Someone had destroyed the work that we had done the night before. There was no hole under the fence. Mother had to search diligently for another opening and then dig our way under again.

Mother did not even bother to climb an apple tree to check if the apples were setting. Instead we went directly to the plywood frame and Mother began to size up how one might gain admittance beyond the wire mesh.

It seemed to take her an awfully long time to find a way. She tried this and that, climbing, twisting, gnawing, pulling. Finally I had decided that there was no way we could get beyond the barrier. Already the night was far spent and we hadn't done any feeding. Soon we would need to get back to the safety of a tree again.

My stomach was growling and my tongue longed for the freshness of the salt. I knew that if Mother and I couldn't find our way to the tasty salt, there was no use even thinking of trying to bring some of it to the other forest creatures. I wouldn't have a feast - and I wouldn't have a friend either.

I felt so discouraged that I wanted to curl right up and cry.

As I was about to do just that, I heard a strange thump and opened my eyes wide to see Mother on the inside of the enclosure.

"How'd you get in there?" I asked excitedly.

For a moment she did not answer. She appeared to have had the wind knocked out of her when she landed on the ground. She lay there, looking at me, blinking her eyes and trying to catch her breath again.

"I . . . I'm not sure," she finally replied. Then a new thought brought her eyes wide open.

"But I know one thing. I've got to find my way out before morning comes. The dogs are bound . . ." She didn't finish her statement but I could see the fear in her eyes.

I began to shake. If Mother didn't know how she got in, then how was she ever to find her way out again? I began to look around me. How would we ever get her out?

"Did you climb in?" I asked nervously.

"I . . . I think I . . ." Mother looked at the wire mesh that stretched up above her head.

"Can't you just climb out?" I had forgotten all about my hunger for the salt. All I could think of now was trying to get Mother out before morning came. Before the dogs began their daily patrols. Before the farmer decided it was time to come to the orchard.

"I . . . I don't know," said Mother.

"But you *must* try," I prompted, casting a glance at the sky. I knew that we didn't have much time.

Mother shook herself and began to look around her.

"Try over there," I encouraged, thinking that the wire looked a bit lower in the far corner.

Mother followed my prompting but it was easy to see that she wouldn't be able to climb out over the wire mesh - not even in the lower corner.

"Can't you just lift yourself up step by step?" I asked her.

Mother tried. It didn't work well at all.

"We'll have to dig me out," she said at last.

"But it will take too long," I reminded her. "The sun will soon be up."

"Maybe I can hide," said Mother. "There is an overhang on that one corner of the frame. Maybe I can squeeze under there and wait until night comes again."

"But what will *I* do?" I began to ask, the tears making my voice shaky.

"You'll have to go back to the forest, dear, and wait until the day has ended and night . . ."

"But what if they find you?" I argued.

"I'll do my best to hide."

"But the dogs? And the farmer?"

Mother looked up at the sky.

"They'll be around anytime now," Mother said simply, making me shiver with the thought of it. "You must get back to the forest."

"But I can't leave you," I began, whimpering in my fright.

"You *must*," said Mother. "You must. You are not safe here."

"But I don't want to go alone," I argued.

I was afraid to be by myself. I had never been all alone before.

"You must be calm," said Mother. "You know what to do. Find yourself a good, safe tree and climb until you are a good distance from the ground. Then pick a spot among the branches where you will be hard to see and settle in for a day's nap. I will hide under the ledge. When night comes, I will look for a way out."

"But . . ." I still hated the thought of being separated from Mother.

"Now you must hurry," said Mother.

"But . . ." I said again.

Then I heard it. The faint stirring and whining of the dogs.

"They are coming," said Mother. "Run! And if you can't outrun them, remember - curl - point - and prepare your tail."

I didn't wait to hear more. I started for the fence as quickly as my legs could carry me.

I could hear the sniffing of the dogs across the

orchard. I knew that they had picked up a scent. Perhaps my scent. Were they headed in my direction?

I heard sharp barking. The dogs were after something.

"Oh, dear," I cried. "They have found me. They'll catch me."

I rushed headlong toward the fence. In my hurry I became confused and couldn't remember where the hole under the fence was located. I felt panic gripping me. They would find me. I would be forced to curl, point my quills and prepare my tail for striking. I was just sure that in my fright I would forget what Mother had taught me.

Behind me I could hear the dogs. They were running now and their barking had become excited.

"This way. This way," I heard the one call to the other.

"What is it?" the other dog asked, his yaps sharp and staccato in their eagerness.

"A woodchuck, I think," came the reply.

"Oh, dear," I cried. "They'll get me for sure. They'll not even stop to discover that I'm a porcupine and have quills until . . . until it is too late."

I cast a glance over my shoulder. Two big creatures with long, lolling tongues, sharp flickering eyes and wide-open mouths were not far behind me. They ran close to one another, right down the path that I was following. I could tell that they were much faster than I. I would never, never make it to the hole in the fence.

I began to cry. I didn't even dare to look back again. I focused on the fence before me and the hole that I was seeking and I hurried as fast as my stubby legs would carry me. I was sure that those sharp teeth would soon be sinking themselves into one of my hind legs. I wouldn't even have time to curl or . . .

To my surprise the running feet turned aside and hurried off down another path.

"There he is," I heard the bigger, brown dog call to the smaller, spotted one. "Over there."

The noise increased as they rushed on.

I couldn't resist turning to look.

"That's not a woodchuck," the little dog called to his partner. "That's a weasel."

"Watch out for his teeth," admonished the bigger dog. "They bite something awful."

I reached the fence, scooted along it until I came to the opening and pushed my way under. I wanted to just lie right there, panting for breath, trying to regain my composure, but I didn't dare. I knew that those dogs were still chasing about in the orchard and Mother had warned me that there were gates for letting creatures in and out.

At the thought of Mother, fear made me tremble again. Oh, I hoped that she would be able to push herself far enough under the overhang to hide from probing eyes.

With a little cry I pulled myself to my feet and hurried off down the makeshift path to find safety in the trees.

I wasn't too choosy. As soon as I spotted a tree that I felt was tall enough and sturdy enough to support one rather small porcupine, I began climbing. My legs still shook and my whole body trembled with fright.

Behind me I could hear the dogs again and I knew

they had left the orchard and were moving my way. Up the tree I went. Not fast, but certainly much faster than I had ever climbed a tree before.

I glanced down at the path that ran beneath me just in time to see a weasel go scurrying by and dive into a hollow log. So there *had* been a weasel. I realized that I might owe that weasel my life. If he hadn't also been in the orchard . . . If he hadn't distracted the dogs . . . I hated to think about it.

The dogs were close behind the weasel. They seemed terribly angry when they reached the log.

"He went in here," shouted the small dog.

"Go in after him," said the big fellow.

The little dog looked like he was going to try. He went to the mouth of the log and pushed himself as far into the opening as he could. But only his head would fit. He barked and shoved and growled at the weasel, but it really did little good.

I had never seen an animal act so ferocious. It made me tremble even as I clung to the tree. I wanted Mother. With all of my heart I wanted her.

Then I thought of her predicament. Would she really be safe in the orchard? Would the dogs return and tear at the plywood frame as they were now digging and ripping at the hollow log? The very thought made me shiver.

I clung to the tree and cried silently. I had never felt so alone in my whole life. I had never *been* so alone in my whole life. And it was all my fault. It was all because I had wanted more of the tasty salt. All because I hoped that I could find some way to share the treat and earn a friendship. I was so sorry. So sorry that I had jeopardized my life - and Mother's life - by talking her into another trip to the orchard. It was just for the sake of satisfying my yearning for a salt treat and, even worse, dreaming my crazy dreams of hopefully earning a friend.

# Chapter Eight

# *Mother*

I awoke early that evening. I hadn't been able to sleep well. Stirring restlessly, I would awaken and find myself whimpering in my sleep. Sometimes it took me a minute to remember what was wrong. At other times, I woke with a start, the knowledge that Mother was not with me very heavy on my mind. Whether I had to slowly sort through my predicament or awoke fully aware that I was by myself and afraid, the results were always the same. I felt dreadfully alone and scared.

What about Mother? Had she been able to hide from the keen noses of the farm dogs and the sharp eyes of the farmer? I trembled every time I thought about what could have happened since I had left her in the orchard.

I knew that I must not leave the safety of the tree until the day had ended but it was all I could do to wait.

I was dreadfully hungry. Mother and I had very little to fill our stomachs the night before. Now another long day had passed and my tummy was telling me that it did not want to be neglected again.

I didn't have time to eat. I had to travel back to the orchard and see if I could find some way to help Mother escape from her terrible predicament.

I grabbed a few quick bites of tree bark as I waited

for the sun to set behind the distant hills. As soon as I heard the soft call of the night owl, I knew that it was time for me to be stirring. I eased my way down the tree, trying hard to remember all of Mother's cautions before I lowered myself to the ground.

I was trembling. My whole body was shaking. It was so frightening to be entirely on my own.

I had taken only a few steps when I heard a rustling in the grasses. I froze - sure that the next sight to greet my eyes would be a pair of blazing eyes, a long, lolling tongue and huge, ragged teeth belonging to a coyote or a bear.

I shut my eyes and instinctively began to curl up tightly.

"Hi," a small, quavering voice said.

I opened my eyes to see a small wood mouse. She stood in the path directly in front of me and her tiny body trembled with her fright.

"I . . . I do hope I haven't disturbed you," she whispered in panic. "I . . . I was just running to . . ."

I let out the air I had been holding.

"Oh, no," I replied quickly. She was shaking as much as I was. "I . . . I was just going to . . . to see my . . ."

"I won't keep you," replied the little mouse. "I'll . . . I'll just . . ."

With a quick flick of her tail she dived back into the grasses and disappeared right before my eyes.

I wanted to call after her. I wanted to talk to her. But she was gone. The first forest creature that I had ever spoken to and she was gone. I felt sad. I roused from where I cowered and tried to shake off my disappoint-

ment. I had to go find Mother.

It was difficult finding the right path that led to the orchard. The night was cool, dark and windy. The moon hid behind scuttling clouds and the smell of rain was in the air. I feared that before morning came, I would be wet to the skin. I hated being wet. My long hair became so heavy that I could hardly move. I decided I'd better hurry before traveling became impossible.

At last I found the right path and reached the fence that shut all creatures out of the orchard. I remembered where Mother had found the place to dig an opening under the fence and headed directly to the spot. But I could have cried when I reached it. The farmer had covered it over again.

I couldn't understand why he kept filling in the entrances. Didn't he know how difficult it was for us to find another way? Now it would take precious time trying to gain an entrance when every second counted. I had to find Mother. I had to help her as quickly as possible.

It was a new experience for me to explore ways to get beyond the big wire fence. Mother seemed to have a special knack for finding a weakness in the structure. I looked and looked and looked. I dug and pushed and pulled and shook but the solid fence did not cooperate. I was still on the outside and Mother was somewhere on the inside.

I had traveled almost all of the way around the fence before I finally found a promising spot. The wire seemed to sag a bit. It appeared that some other animal had been working on it. In fact, I found as I looked more closely, some very little creature had dug himself under the fence.

Immediately I became excited. If one animal had already gone under, then surely I could. Shoving my nose under the wire, I began to push. I knew at once that my large body was not going to slip under the fence through the opening used by a weasel or a small rabbit.

Although I was very disappointed, I decided to settle down and make the opening larger. I set to work.

It was slow digging. I kept running into tree roots and small rocks and had to work my way around them or remove them. One tree root seemed to take forever to chew my way through. One small rock refused to budge and I had to dig around it.

At last the opening was big enough for me to squeeze through. I pushed my head under, wriggled my body to follow and began to push my way through to the other side of the fence.

The opening wasn't quite as large as I had thought it to be. Unexpectedly my body wedged itself tightly under the middle of the fence.

I panicked. I was stuck. I would never get out. The dogs would find me half in and half out of the orchard. I had seen them dig at the hollow log in their wild effort to reach the weasel. I had no trouble picturing what it would be like when they found me in such a precarious position.

I tried to back out. I could not budge. I pushed myself forward. I could not move. I struggled and fought, panic making me squirm and press against the ground under me. I was stuck fast.

In my fright I began to whimper. What would I do?

What would I ever do?

I thought that I heard something coming. Whether it was the wind in the tree boughs or something really stirring in the orchard I did not know. All I knew was that it frightened me so badly that I thought my heart would surely burst with its wild beating.

"It's coming. It's coming," I said to myself. "And I can't move. I can't even curl."

I knew that I was doomed. I closed my eyes tightly and waited for the sharp crunch of the wicked teeth as the creature reached out for me.

Several minutes ticked slowly by and nothing happened. I waited, my heart thumping within me. Still nothing happened.

Finally, I drew in a deep breath and forced myself to open my eyes. Before me lay the orchard, the tall grasses at the foot of the apple trees shivering in the night wind. Overhead a small sliver of moon peeked out from a cloud for one brief moment and then tucked in behind another.

"Even the moon does not want to look," I said to myself.

Suddenly the very thing that I had dreaded began to happen. It started to rain. Softly at first came big splashy drops that slapped on my nose and pinged on the wire fence. I blinked hard against it. It was bad enough to be out in the rain but even worse when one could not move at all to protect oneself.

The rain came faster. Huge drops splattered as they landed on me and about me. I hated it. I could not even curl up to protect myself. I was held a prisoner as it pelted all around me. I couldn't imagine being more miserable.

There was nothing that I could do. I just shut my eyes and let the horrid water beat against my unprotected body. I could feel the water puddling beneath me. Soon, what had been hard ground a few moments before, was quickly becoming squishy mud. I hated it. I hated it with all of my being.

"I've got to get out of this mess," I said to myself, gritting my teeth and digging my long paw nails into the soggy earth beneath me. "I've got to. I'll drown if I don't."

I gave a giant push with both of my hind paws and was surprised to feel something slipping under me. "I think I moved a little bit," I said to myself excitedly and prepared for another big shove.

It took a lot of pushing and shoving. Soon I was panting and my body was warm again from the exertion. Little by little, I began to shove myself clear of the wire fence that held me prisoner. At last, with a funny little thump, I flopped free and lay puffing, trying to get my breath and my bearings at the same time.

"I'm out," I managed to whisper. "I'm out."

For one moment I could not even move. I was too tired from all of the pushing and panting. I lay there with the rain still beating against me. My coat was soggy and dirty and weighed a ton.

"I've got to find Mother," I reminded myself and pushed slowly to my feet. Shaking the water from my coat as best I could, I started down the path before me. I had lost track of where I was and had no idea which way to travel. Where was the plywood frame and the wire enclosure that had imprisoned Mother? I would just have to keep on looking until I found it.

Several paths I tried seemed to lead nowhere. I was beginning to despair. At this rate I would never find Mother. The night was passing quickly. The orchard paths were getting wetter and more slippery with the pelting rain. In some places I had to wade through several inches of water. I hated it but I didn't know how to avoid it.

I didn't dare call for Mother. The farm dogs might hear me. So I just kept walking and looking, seeming to go around and around in senseless circles.

At last, when I was about to give up, the strange frame construction suddenly loomed up before me through the misty rain. I ran forward and pushed my nose up against the wire.

"Mother!" I cried, my voice louder than I had intended it to be. "Mother! Where are you?"

Everything was silent and I felt the fear start my heart thumping again. Was she gone? Had they found her? Would I ever see my Mother again?

Then a soft whisper answered me, "Pordy? Pordy, is that you?"

She sounded as if she had been aroused from sleeping.

"Mother?"

There was a stirring then. Soon Mother's nose was pressed against the wire enclosure. "Oh, I'm glad you've come," she said. "I had quite given up."

"I . . . I was stuck . . . for hours . . . under the fence. I couldn't get in and I couldn't get out," I tried to explain.

"Well, no matter now," said Mother with urgency

affecting her voice. "We must get me out. I've looked and looked and I haven't found a way."

"Maybe if we . . ." I pushed against the fence with all of my heavy little body. It did not budge.

"I think we'll just have to dig our way," said Mother. "I've got a hole started over here but the rain . . ."

I knew all about the rain.

"If we can work together . . ." said Mother.

"We'll get you out, Mother," I said with more conviction than I felt. "We will. We just have to."

"There's a soft spot here," said Mother. "Let's try to dig. You work from out there and I'll . . ." She stopped talking and started to dig. I began at once to dig on the outside.

The rain did not seem to slacken. It beat down on my head and splashed over my nose. It soaked my coat and made the ground slippery under my paws. It whipped against the plywood frame and dripped down the wire mesh. Mother and I tried to ignore it as we worked furiously. We had to get her out before another morning arrived. We absolutely had to.

## Chapter Nine

## *The Misadventure*

If the rain had stopped and the clouds had blown away, the sun would have been up again before we finally managed to free Mother from the wire enclosure. As it was, it was still quite dark and dreary and the creatures of the farm did not seem anxious to be stirring about. I did not even hear the dogs. For that I was most thankful.

"I think I can push my way through, now," Mother exclaimed at last.

"Don't get stuck," I cautioned, recalling the helpless feeling of not being able to go ahead or go back.

Mother wriggled her way into the mud under the wire and pushed hard with her hind claws. I saw her inch forward little by little. I held my breath. At one point, I was sure that she was going to get stuck and be held captive under the wire mesh. With one mammoth push, she managed to get her body wriggling through again and I stepped back and let out the breath I had been holding.

She finally pulled herself free and eased her body up through the mud. We were both a terrible mess but I was so glad to see her. So glad to be able to reach out and press my nose against hers and welcome her into the clear again.

My triumph over her escape was short-lived as Mother reminded me, "Now we have to get ourselves out of this orchard."

"How did you come in?" she asked. I was afraid that she would ask me that. The truth was, I had no idea which path led to the opening under the fence.

"I . . . I don't know. I don't think . . ." I responded in a whisper. "I can't remember."

"Well, no matter," said Mother simply. "We'll just have to look until we find it," and she started off down an orchard path. I wanted to call after her, "I don't think it's that way," but I didn't. After all, I had totally lost my bearings. I had no idea which way we should go. Though I didn't feel right about the way Mother was heading, I had no idea what direction to take. I shook some of the heavy rain from my coat and followed along behind her.

It took us a long while to find the hole under the fence. By now the entrance was not just soggy and muddy - it was completely under water. I knew that Mother wouldn't like slithering in the dirty puddles any more than I did. I wondered what we should do now.

As Mother hesitated, I found my voice.

"What do we do?" I asked shakily.

"We've got to get out of here," she answered matter-of-factly, as she edged toward the flooded entrance and took a deep breath. Then she surprised me by turning to me.

"You'd better go first," she told me. "You've been through once so we know you'll fit under. I don't wish to get stuck and block your exit."

I looked at her, my eyes wild with fright. I had been under the fence once - but I had just barely made it. Mother was still a good deal larger than I. Was there a chance that she could make it through the opening? I wasn't sure. We needed a bigger hole under the fence. I just knew we did.

"You'll never make it, Mother," I said in a worried whisper. "I hardly made it. I was stuck for hours. Then I was just able to wriggle my way out."

"We don't have time to dig another," said Mother simply.

"We have to," I insisted. "You'll get stuck for sure. The dogs will . . ."

I felt terror gripping me. I couldn't leave Mother behind again. I just couldn't. This time, there wouldn't even be an overhang under which she could hide. She would be exposed for the farmer and his dogs to see - or else she would drown in the puddles that were getting deeper and deeper by the minute.

I looked wildly around us. There had to be another way. It was far too risky for Mother to try to crawl out under the fence.

My eyes traveled down the length of wire. It looked solid and stretched on and on as far as my eyes could see in both directions and then . . . then the strangest, most welcome sight met my eyes.

"Mother! Look!" I cried, pointing to the west. "Look! The gate is open."

Sure enough. Someone had been through the orchard gate and left it swinging wide open.

"Well, would you look at that!" said Mother in disbelief.

As she spoke, she was moving toward the gate as though afraid that something would reach out and close it again.

I hurried after her. I did not wish to be left behind.

The wind was swinging the gate back and forth, back and forth on complaining hinges. I watched Mother start through when the gate opened wide enough to allow her passage. She was still moving through when the gate swung around, thumping her loudly on her soggy side. I heard her grunt and mutter under her breath. I stopped right where I was. The gate was almost closed now and I feared that it would not open again for me.

"Hurry, dear," I heard Mother say, but I still hesitated.

Another gust of wind swung the gate open but, before I could move forward, it had swung back again. I wanted to cry. We were separated again. Mother was now on the outside of the fence and I was still on the inside.

But Mother did not desert me. I saw her press her nose against the wire mesh of the fence.

"When it swings open, dear," she said, "push your way through."

"It might hit me," I whined.

"It won't hurt you even if it does," said Mother. "It just pushes you through a bit faster."

"But I . . ." I began.

"Be ready when it swings open again," said Mother firmly.

I braced myself, waiting for another gust of the wind.

The rain was still falling and dripping off the end of my nose.

As soon as the gate began to swing open, I heard Mother call softly, "Get ready now, Pordy."

I got ready to make my awkward dash through the partly opened gate.

"Now!" said Mother with a great deal of urgency.

I moved forward. The gate moved, too, and I snubbed my nose directly into one of the wooden boards. With a sharp cry, I backed away. My timing had been off.

"We must hurry," I heard Mother say. She was getting most anxious to be away from the orchard.

I prepared myself again and waited for the wind to swing the gate open. It appeared that the gate was not going to open for me again. Mother soon took matters into her own paws. She moved to the gate and pushed against it with her nose. "Wiggle your way through, Pordy," she advised me.

I stepped over to the gate. There was just enough of an opening to shove my nose through. As I pushed against the gate, the opening narrowed again. I almost got my nose caught as the gate swung shut.

"Not like that, dear," said Mother. "You must push your nose through and open the gate wider. Don't push against the gate from your side. Let your nose push back against this side of the gate."

I tried it again. Mother pushed the gate far enough for me to get my nose through it again. Then I twisted my head and pushed the gate back in the direction of my body.

Slowly the gap began to widen. With Mother's help from the other side I was able to get the gate open wide enough to move my body forward. It still didn't seem to be working well. I was about to give up when another gust of wind wrenched the gate from me and flung it open wide. The sudden jolt sent me sprawling into the mud of the path. I didn't want to miss the opportunity so I clambered quickly to my feet and pushed myself forward before the gate could blow shut again.

"Good," said Mother when I fell at her feet in the mud. "You are through."

Just in time, too. Right behind me there was another loud clang as the wind blew the gate shut once again.

We were safe now. Both Mother and I were outside the enclosure. We were free to head back to the safety of our tree home.

Mother led the way and I followed along after her. We couldn't really hurry. Already slow by nature, we were even slower now. Our coats were heavy with rainwater and mud. Our stomachs were empty because we had not eaten. And we were extremely tired from the big chore of getting ourselves back outside the fence of the orchard.

But we were relieved. It was wonderful to be free again. Quietly we trudged toward home. Suddenly a thought hit me. I had missed out on the wonderful salt treat. I was sure that Mother must have had plenty of time to enjoy all of the salt she wanted.

"Did you get some salt?" I asked her.

She seemed to hesitate mid-stride. "Salt?" she asked as though she didn't understand what I was talking about.

"Salt," I said simply. "From the plywood."

"Oh, salt. No. No, I didn't eat any salt."

"But why?"

"I was much too concerned about staying hidden from the dogs. And the farmer spent most of the day in the orchard. I didn't want him to spot me. I just hid under the overhang and kept as quiet as I could."

It didn't sound like Mother had spent a very good day, either.

"And besides," continued Mother slowly, "I was worried about you. I was afraid that . . ."

"I was fine," I cut in quickly. "I spent all day up in a tree. I didn't come down until it got dark - just like you taught me."

"I'm proud of you, dear," said Mother.

I felt a little - just a teeny, little bit - proud of me, too. I felt my face grow warm. But it was a rather nice glow. Then I thought of something else.

"You know what?" I said excitedly. "When I was on my way to the orchard, I heard something coming through the grass. I was scared at first. I thought it might be a coyote or a bear or . . . or almost anything. But it wasn't. It was just a little wood mouse and . . . and she stopped right still and she looked scared and shaky but then . . . then she talked to me. She said she was sorry."

"Sorry?" said Mother. "Why sorry?"

"I don't really know. I guess she thought I would be upset about her almost running into me."

"What did you say?" asked Mother.

"I started to say it was okay but she didn't wait to talk. She just ran."

"That's too bad," said Mother and I knew that she understood how important it was to me to talk to someone.

I nodded my head slowly.

"I wanted so much to talk to her," I admitted.

We walked along for a few seconds. Each one of us was busy with our own thoughts. Then I spoke again.

"Mother, why wouldn't the mouse wait to talk to me?" I asked.

I thought that I had already figured out the reason, but I hoped Mother would come up with a different one.

Mother seemed to be thinking about my question. When she answered she sounded a bit uncertain.

"I don't know," she replied.

"Didn't she like me?" I asked soberly, sure that was the answer to my question.

"She doesn't know you, dear," said Mother.

"I know. But doesn't she like me?"

"You can't not-like a person you don't know, dear," said Mother.

"Then why did she run?"

Mother stopped and waited for me to come puffing up beside her on the trail. Then she answered my question quietly. "Perhaps she was just in a hurry, dear," she said.

I thought about that. The wood mouse did seem to be in a dreadful hurry all right.

"Or," Mother went on, "perhaps she was frightened."

"Frightened?" I parroted, "I wouldn't have hurt her. I'm not a fox or a coyote or a . . ."

"But she didn't know you," said Mother. "Sometimes it is easy to be frightened of things we don't know. And one does have to be careful, dear. I'm sure that her mother has told her not to chat with forest strangers.''

"I wish she would have waited for me to explain,'' I said. "I would have told her that I . . .''

"And then again,'' Mother cut in, "she might have just been shy.''

"Shy?''

"Like you, Pordy,'' explained Mother. "You are shy. Too shy to try to make friends with the other little animals.''

I hung my head. I knew that I was shy but I had a good reason. All the other forest creatures already had their friends and families. I knew that they wouldn't want to be approached by a spiny porcupine. It wasn't only because I was shy. It was also because I didn't want them to tease me or turn their backs on me or tell me that they didn't want to play with me. It wasn't the same as it was with me and the little wood mouse. Not the same at all.

# Chapter Ten

# *A Way In*

It took most of the day for Mother and I to dry out. The rain didn't stop but we were able to find a nice sheltered spot in our tree where we were out of the wind. We curled up closely against the trunk and slept in spite of our discomfort. By the time evening came again, my fur felt quite comfortable but my stomach did not. Never do I remember feeling quite so hungry.

"Mother," I prompted. "Mother, I'm starved."

Mother awoke slowly and lifted her head to look down at me. She yawned and stretched but did not answer.

"I'm starved," I said again, impatience edging my voice.

"Yes," she answered slowly. "It has been a long time since we've had a good meal."

"Where will we eat?" I asked, anxious to get started. It was getting dark. The clouds had hidden the sun all day and now were making no room for the moon to shine either.

"I think right here," said Mother.

"Here?"

"There is plenty to eat right here. I see no reason to drag ourselves through the mud. Yes, we'll eat right here.''

I was too hungry to argue. Besides I hated the thought of the wet paths. Moving out from my position near the trunk of the tree, I began climbing slowly. I knew that the best eating was near the top.

We didn't talk much as we fed. There didn't seem to be much to talk about. Besides, we were both too hungry to spend time in idle chatter. We just ate and ate.

It was quiet and still in the forest that night. Even the night birds seemed reluctant to stir about. I didn't hear any chattering of rabbits or stirring of skunks. The squirrels went to bed early, without even arguing over the fact.

Since there was nothing to distract me, I just ate on and on, trying my best to stay as dry as I could. It was hard to do because it was still raining and, being higher in the tree, I was less sheltered than I had been while I slept.

''That feels much better, doesn't it?'' Mother asked, breaking the silence. It was the first that either of us had spoken for several hours.

I lifted my head, realizing that I was really quite full. Full and contented. We had been feeding all night. In the east, a faint glow lightened the sky. It would soon be morning again.

''I think the sun may shine today,'' observed Mother. ''The rain has stopped but the clouds are still in the sky. Perhaps they will move away now.''

Her comment surprised me. I hadn't realized that the rain had stopped. Because my coat was still so wet and heavy, I had not noticed the storm moving on.

It was nice to have the rain over. Even as I thought about it, I felt the wind stirring my long fur. Without the rain pelting us, we would soon be dry again. I was pleased about that. I didn't like the feel of rain on my back.

"I think we should get a good sleep now," said Mother. "We will sleep much better today with a nice full stomach."

I agreed for I hadn't slept well over the past day. Nor the day before that when I had been separated from Mother. It would take another good sleep or two for me to catch up again.

I did not argue with Mother. Slowly I backed down the tree until I was in a cozier position. Tucking myself in close to the trunk and curling up tightly, I was ready for another long nap. Even the noisy jays and chattering squirrels failed to rouse me as I slept on and on.

When I woke again, the clouds had disappeared and the evening sun was just touching the last of the treetops with its warm golden rays. To the east the moon was climbing, its round, full orb changing from gold to silver as the sun slipped out of sight. It looked as if it would be a glorious night.

I was still yawning and stretching when I heard a clamor down below. I looked down to see what the fuss was about. Jugsy Rabbit was standing on a small mound beneath our tree, waving his arms excitedly and calling to the squirrel triplets up among the branches.

"Can you stay out and play for a while? It's a beautiful evening. We can play Hide and Seek."

Around Jugsy gathered Tugsy and Topsy and three other rabbits. Off to the side two skunk children waited.

One was Freddie but I didn't know the other. Even Spoof was there and he had another woodchuck with him. All of the forest young were anxious for a game after being shut in by rain for the past couple of days.

I had been hungry again when I first awoke but now the sight below drove all thought of eating from me. I shifted my position in the tree so that I could watch the game more closely.

"We can't play long," called Millicent Squirrel. "Mother says it is almost bedtime."

"Then we need to start," said Tugsy.

A chorus of, "Not it. Not it," rang through the woods. Spoof was declared "it" and the game began with the new skunk that I didn't know posted as first sentry.

Mother had climbed higher into our tree and began her evening feeding. I knew that I should be eating, too, but I just couldn't take my eyes off the scene below.

Spoof moved up to our tree trunk and placed his paws over his eyes. I heard him counting loudly. All the other little animals seemed to melt into the forest trees. Soon Spoof was the only animal that I could see. Where had the others gone? Would Spoof be angry at being left all alone?

Then Spoof called out loudly, "Here I come. Ready or not." He left his spot and began to peek and poke among the underbrush.

He had gone only a few steps from the tree when Jugsy sneaked in behind him and cried loudly, "Home free."

Spoof turned quickly and dashed for the tree trunk but he was too late to catch Jugsy.

He began to look through the forest bushes again. The other woodchuck was the next one to make his appearance. He sneaked around the tree trunk from the back and shouted, "Home free," as well. Spoof came running but the other woodchuck beat him to the tree.

Again Spoof went looking. This time it was Topsy who popped up. She tried to get to the tree first but Spoof was there ahead of her. "One, two, three on Topsy," he called. Topsy giggled. She had been caught.

One by one all of the other forest young were found or caught trying to make a dash for the tree. Soon it was time for the game to start over. Topsy took her place at the tree trunk as she covered her eyes with her paws and counted loudly. Spoof joined the others as they scattered about the forest, hiding under bushes, behind shrubbery, in hollow logs and among rocks. Rodney Squirrel climbed to a tree branch to take his turn as sentry.

From my spot in the tree I watched the game. Excitement filled me each time I saw another player come sneaking toward the tree trunk. One time I almost called out to warn Millicent, who was "it," that someone was coming. I quickly bit my lip. I would have spoiled the game and embarrassed myself dreadfully.

All too soon Mrs. Squirrel called in her young and, with their number missing, the other forest children scattered to their homes. I knew some of them needed to eat. They were night creatures - not day creatures like the squirrels - and they had to spend their time feeding before the sun made its appearance again.

Suddenly I realized that I was also hungry. An hour

of my feeding time had already passed. Mother had been feeding. She looked quite content as she nibbled away at the tender bark high up in the branches.

"I was thinking," she observed as she chewed, "with the rain still softening the ground, it would be much easier to dig."

I didn't know what she meant by her statement so I began to munch on my tree bark.

"I suppose we could make a trip back to the orchard," Mother went on.

My head came up then. I hadn't forgotten how nice the salt had tasted. Mother and I had been thwarted on our last trip. I knew that we'd both enjoy a good feed on the salt. And I had to find some way to bring a salt treat back for the other young animals.

"Have you had enough to eat yet?" asked Mother.

I had only had a few bites but I didn't want to wait until I had eaten. "I'm ready," I said with no hesitation.

Mother nodded her head and we both began to back slowly down the tree.

"I wonder if I might meet the little wood mouse again," I thought excitedly as we began our journey down the forest path. All the way to the orchard I kept watching and listening but there was no sign of any other little creature.

When we reached the high fence, Mother began searching for a way in. The first thing we did was seek out the gate just in case the wind had left it open. We found it closed tightly, much to our disappointment. We hurried on to look for another way in.

It didn't take Mother long to find a way under the

fence. We scrambled over the orchard trails and made our way to the plywood frame. It was still enclosed within the wire mesh. Mother didn't hesitate for one second. She began to climb and search and try first this approach and then that. I didn't see how it happened - but there she was on the inside of the enclosure again. She hadn't even fallen with a thump.

"Climb up that nearby apple tree, dear," she whispered to me. "That one limb has been broken by the wind and hangs right over the frame."

I looked to where Mother was pointing and, sure enough, the limb reached right over the frame and inside the enclosure. It would be no problem at all to climb up the tree, out on the limb and step right off onto the plywood. I licked my lips as I hurried after Mother.

We had a delightful feed of salt. We had to chew up quite a large area of the plywood to get at the salt but it was well worth the trouble. I was disappointed that I had not discovered a way to share the salt and make friends, but I brushed the thought aside with a deep sigh. I was more than ready to go looking for a water supply again.

"Shall we go back to the stream?" I asked Mother. "I'm thirsty."

"We should be able to find water much closer than that," said Mother. I had forgotten all of the nice puddles that the rain had left behind.

Mother lifted herself from the plywood frame back up onto the tree limb and I followed her lead. It was much easier to climb the apple tree branch and back down the trunk than to dig our way under the wire. I smiled to myself in the darkness. I was glad Mother had found this easy way to get at the salt snack.

"Can we come again tonight?" I asked Mother as we hurried under the high wire fence and away from the orchard.

Mother nodded.

I began to think of the woodland creatures. Maybe I would be able to bring some salt to them or bring them to the salt. If I could do that, I was sure that I could make a friend. Maybe even many friends. I didn't tell Mother about my plan because she might not think it was a good idea.

We found a clean puddle of clear, cool water and stopped to drink our fill before returning to our home in the tree. As I curled up and prepared for a good day's sleep, I thought again of the salt and how easy it was to reach it now. A sleepy smile flitted across my face in the darkness. I could hardly wait for the day to pass and the evening to come again.

# Chapter Eleven

## *The Trap*

That evening I was so excited about going back to the orchard that I didn't even take time to watch the game being played below us. Mother said that we should eat a good feeding of bark before leaving our tree and so I set right to work.

There were times when the game became especially exciting and I couldn't help but look at what was going on. But, for the most part, I fed steadily.

I had decided that I would find some way to bring a portion of the plywood back to the forest with me. My plan was all worked out. After bringing it to our forest area, I would place the plywood where the young forest creatures could easily find it. Perhaps at the base of our tree where they always gathered for their evening game. When they found the treat they'd all look around and say, "Where did this come from?" I would wait a few minutes and then say quietly, "I brought it." Then one of them would say, "Is it yours?" and I would answer, just as quietly, "I brought it for all of you."

I could just picture their eyes as they looked first at the piece of plywood and then at me in the tree. I wouldn't be too high up in the branches because I would want to see the smiles on their faces. I would also want to be near enough for them to invite me down to share in their game. They would look at me, smile slowly and say real loud so that all of the forest creatures could hear, "How nice of you to think of us. Won't you come join our game?"

It was there that my planning had stopped. Even the thought of being asked to join them made my face feel hot. Of course, I knew that I would join them. They would all be so happy to have me for their friend and I would never need to be alone again.

But first I had to discover a way to get a piece of that plywood back to the forest.

I was sure that Mother would know how to accomplish it but I didn't wish to ask her. What if she thought that it was silly? I decided to find a way to do it on my own.

But first - first, we had to reach the orchard again and find the apple trees. It would be a simple thing to climb out on the branch and into the enclosure with the plywood frame. Of course, Mother and I would both chew until our own needs had been met, then I would find a way to claim a big piece of the plywood for my new friends. I knew that it would not be easy to chew off a chunk. But it was possible. Nor would it be easy to drag the piece back to the forest. What most concerned me was getting it under the fence. I hoped that the wind had opened the gate again.

But the gate was still firmly closed when we reached the orchard. We had to find a spot to squeeze under the wire.

When at last we had gained access, we made our way through the trees and over to the plywood frame.

Mother climbed up the apple tree first and I was close behind her. She started right for the limb that hung out over the enclosure. But she stopped short.

"What is it?" I asked as my nose bumped into the back end of her.

"The limb," said Mother.

"What's wrong with it?" I asked, concern in my voice.

"It's gone," said Mother

"Gone? Gone where?"

"I don't know, dear," said Mother, "but it's gone."

"But it can't be," I insisted as I looked past Mother to where the limb had been. It was true. It was gone. There was nothing there. Absolutely nothing but a dark patch with some smelly stuff on the side of the tree where the broken limb had been.

"It must be the farmer," said Mother. "He always ruins things."

I couldn't imagine why the farmer would spoil a perfectly good entrance into the enclosure. It was by far the best way we had found yet and now it was gone.

"What will we do?" I asked Mother, a sob in my voice.

"We'll have to find another way," said Mother simply. She turned and was about to back down the tree when she stopped short. I heard her rummaging around in the dark and then I heard her smacking.

"What is it?" I asked innocently.

"The apples," said Mother. "They are getting bigger."

"But we didn't come for apples," I reminded her.

"True," she said, "but while we are here, we may as

well take advantage of them.''

She continued to chew and smack.

I was a little annoyed but I tried not to let it show. Instead I shifted my weight around to see if I could find one of the apples.

I did, and was pleasantly surprised at the taste. It wasn't long until I had almost forgotten the reason for coming to the orchard. I was enjoying the apple snack as much as I had enjoyed the salt snack the night before.

''We should go,'' said Mother. ''We don't have much time if we plan to find a way into the enclosure again.''

I knew it was true but I hated to leave the apples.

Mother backed down the apple tree and thumped to the ground. I could hear her rummaging around in the darkness. I knew I should follow her. Reluctantly I took one last big bite of apple and began to back down to join her.

''We need to be careful,'' Mother cautioned me. ''The farmer has been around again and one never knows what kind of trap he might invent.''

''Trap?'' I questioned. ''What do you mean, trap?''

''Oh, sometimes he devises ways of catching things. I remember seeing a crow caught in a contraption once. And I've heard the rabbits talk about being caught in a box. You just never know what the farmer might think of next.''

''What happens?'' I asked. ''What happens if one is caught in one of his traps?''

''I don't really know,'' replied Mother. ''I have always avoided them.''

I wished to avoid them as well. But that might be

hard to do if one didn't know what to watch out for.

"Just move carefully," said Mother, "and don't stick your nose into something without being sure of what it is."

Mother's words made me nervous. "Perhaps we should go home," I said.

"We'll look around a little first," she replied. "Can't hurt to just look around."

I followed closely at Mother's heels. I did wish I knew what to watch for.

We neared the plywood frame enclosure and I began to get excited again. Gradually, as we poked and prodded, my fear began to leave me. I almost forgot to be careful as Mother had warned. All I could think of was getting inside to chew the plywood with its salt.

Then I spotted something new. It was made of plywood too, though it did have some wire mesh around it. But the wire did not keep one from reaching the plywood itself. One end was open and from inside was coming the most unusual, but delicious aroma. I hurried toward it.

"Mother," I called back over my shoulder. "Come see. I have found something . . . wonderful."

"What?" called Mother.

"I'm not sure," I replied. "But it smells delicious and it is right here outside the wire and . . ."

I reached out my quivering nose as I leaned forward to step through the small opening.

"Pordy! Stop!" I heard Mother scream behind me and I jerked myself backward just as a door above my head came crashing down. It struck me on the nose as it fell and I reeled back in pain and fright.

Mother pushed up beside me and pushed me further back. "Get away from it, Pordy," she panted, her voice filled with panic.

I was whimpering from my hurt and confusion but I backed away as I had been told.

"It's a trap," said Mother.

"A trap?" I still wasn't sure just what had happened. It had taken me so totally off-guard.

"A trap," Mother repeated again.

"But it is just a . . . an open box," I was foolish enough to argue.

"An open box - with an open invitation," said Mother. "If you would have stepped through that door you would never have stepped out again."

"You mean . . . ?"

"That door was meant to slam down *behind* you," said Mother, "not just catch you on the nose."

"But . . ."

"Oh, yes," continued Mother. "A very clever trap."

"But . . . but there was something in there to eat," I tried to explain to Mother.

"Of course. Food. That's what the farmer always uses to bait his traps - food. He knows that animals are always hungry. He put food in the trap to lure you in. If you had stepped inside, you would have been caught. Caught behind the closed trap door."

The very thought of how close I had been to being caught made me shiver.

"Come," said Mother. "I think we'd better get out of the orchard. There may be other traps around."

Suddenly I was scared. My nose was still smarting

but I knew that I had been very lucky. Mother had warned me about traps and yet I had nearly gotten myself caught in one.

I was shaking so badly that I didn't know if I would be able to follow Mother as she led us from the orchard, but I stumbled after her as quickly as I could.

There would be no plywood treat to share with the woodland creatures. There would be no way for me to make a friend. Why, I was lucky just to be alive and in one piece. I rubbed my nose against my front leg as I walked hurriedly after Mother. I wasn't likely to forget this experience soon. My nose would remind me, if nothing else.

We were just pushing our way out from under the fence when we heard the farm dogs. I didn't even stop to worry about my nose. I tucked my long tail in as close to my shaking body as I could and hurried through the woods after Mother. I was afraid that the dogs had picked up our scent. I guess they had, too, for I could hear them on the other side of the wire fence. They were barking excitedly and making an awful commotion.

It wasn't until we were safely back in the woods that Mother spoke again.

"Perhaps we should stay away from the orchard for a while," she commented.

She didn't say that we would never go back - just that we should stay away for a while.

I agreed with all of my heart. My smarting nose agreed also. I nodded my head in compliance and followed Mother toward our little grove of trees.

"Are you thirsty?" asked Mother.

I didn't really know if I was thirsty or not. But I did know that I was still scared.

All I wanted was to climb a tree and get as high off the ground as my long claws would take me.

I shook my head. "I don't think so," I replied. However, even as I answered Mother, I thought that it would sure feel good to stick my burning nose into some nice, cool water.

I could still hear the dogs baying back at the fence.

"I don't think so," I said again.

"Me either," said Mother. "I think that we should tuck away for the day.

Tuck away. It sounded nice and cozy and safe. It sounded like a wonderful idea.

"Let's," I said. "Let's just tuck away."

We reached our own strand of trees and Mother started up first as she always did. I followed close behind her. I'd had enough adventure for one night and was quite content to snuggle up in one of the overhanging boughs and get some sleep. The trap had frightened me even more than being separated from Mother. I was still trembling.

"Try to get some rest, dear," said Mother softly from her spot just above me.

I nodded. If I could just stop shivering, I might discover that I was tired.

I stuck out my tongue and licked at my sore nose. Yes, it was going to take some time to forget this night's adventure.

Chapter Twelve

# The Garden

We didn't talk about the orchard in the days that followed. I still shivered each time I thought about what could have happened if I had stepped inside that farmer's trap. My nose still smarted if I happened to bump it against something.

Mother and I stayed in our own little grove of trees and ate contentedly of the bark and leaves that they supplied.

I suppose we both thought of the orchard. I still lamented over the fact that I now had no way to win the friendship of the forest young. I rather resigned myself to spending the rest of my life alone with no friend of my very own.

I had given up ever meeting the wood mouse, too. I watched and watched the paths in the woods but I did not spot her again.

I spent many hours watching the other young animals of the forest. They still gathered almost every evening to play games but, as closely as I watched their activities, they never saw me in the boughs above them. At times I was thankful that I could watch them totally unobserved. At other times I wished with all my heart that someone - anyone - would recognize my presence.

One night as I watched the game below, Mother slipped silently up beside me. "Why don't you go down and join them?" she asked me quietly.

I was shocked by her suggestion. I wouldn't even consider joining the group of friends below. I knew that I was different and I was sure that I would not be welcome. Could one imagine a porcupine trying to make a dash for the safety of "home base?" I turned away from Mother to hide my confusion and frustration.

"Don't you want friends?" Mother asked me.

"I . . . I guess not . . . not . . . that much," I replied. "It . . . it takes all my time to . . . to get enough to eat."

What I didn't say was that I would gladly have gone with an empty stomach just to have one friend of my own.

"Eat? Yes. It does take time for us to find enough to eat. I've been thinking, though. There might be easier eating than what we are finding in the treetops."

She had my attention. "Are you thinking of going back to the orchard?" I asked, my voice shaky.

"The orchard? No, I think not. I still feel that it might be a bit risky. However, I do happen to know where there is a nice garden."

"A garden?"

I had heard the rabbits chatter excitedly about a garden. They always spoke as though it was the best eating in the world.

"Where?" I asked.

"To the north," said Mother and my pulse raced faster. The orchard was to the east. We would not need to go anywhere near the trap or the dogs or the farmer.

"Mrs. Tinker always plants a garden. Every year her vegetables are the best in the whole area. I've heard several animals say so. They should be getting big enough to be good and juicy by now."

It sounded very good to me. "Can we go tonight?" I asked Mother.

She nodded her head. "I think it might be time," she responded.

Then I had a new thought and I hesitated just a moment. "Does she set traps?" I asked.

"I've never known her to set a trap," replied Mother. "It seems that she plants enough vegetables to share."

It was sounding better all the time.

"Let's go," I said excitedly. My nose was almost totally healed since my brush with the trap door. It wiggled now in anticipation.

Mother slowly began to climb down from our tree. I followed her, eager to be led to where the nice, juicy vegetables were awaiting us.

As we traveled the forest path, I thought of the other animals. Mother had often heard them speak of Mrs. Tinker's garden. Would there be a chance that we might meet some of the rabbits or some of the skunks in the garden patch? The thought filled me with excitement. I began to daydream again.

This time I was not dragging home some plywood so that I could share a treat. No, this time I was being a heroine of another sort.

I could see myself returning home from the garden spot with Mother. We would be plodding along the path, minding our own business, quietly making our way through the trees of the forest. Just ahead of us on the trail walked a group of rabbits. Of course they were chattering wildly, forgetting that one should always walk the forest paths quietly, ever alert for danger.

Ahead of the rabbits walked the skunk youngsters. They, too, were talking and laughing, paying little attention to dangers that might lurk in the undergrowth.

In front of the skunks were the woodchucks. I had never seen more than two woodchucks in the forest but in my dreams there were six or seven or maybe a dozen woodchucks all traveling together. In the branches along the path, several squirrels frisked back and forth. Occasionally one of them dashed down to the ground to pass on a secret to the marching throng. Never had I seen so many woodland creatures gathered in one place.

Just as we neared the glade, there was a stirring in the underbrush - but no one heard it. No one, that is, except me. The rest had been chatting and teasing but I had been carefully watching the deep shadows, ever alert to the dangers of the woods.

Out from the darkness a slim body emerged. I knew at once that it was a fox. No, a coyote. A coyote was bigger than a fox and thus, I judged, far more dangerous. No, not just one coyote. Two coyotes. Or three. Or a whole pack of coyotes. All with green, glinting eyes and long, drooling tongues and huge, evil-looking teeth.

Of course, no one had seen them. No one but me.

I screamed, "Look out! Coyotes! Look out!"

Of course everyone was terrified. They had been caught off-guard. There wasn't time to hide. There was nowhere to run. The coyotes were all around them.

Someone would be eaten for sure.

That was when I went into action. I sprang forward. I really had to use my imagination here as porcupines are not known to spring forward quickly. I sprang forward and began my attack. Rushing right toward the coyotes, I began lashing my tail this way and that way, delivering stinging blows, with quills flying in every direction, striking coyotes right and left.

Pure pandemonium broke out all around me. The little forest creatures screamed in fright. The coyotes howled with terror and pain. I fought bravely onward, mowing down the enemies before me.

When everything settled down, the coyotes had all gone yelping through the woods, never to come back to our glade again. And I was surrounded by adoring and thankful friends who declared me to be a wonderful heroine who risked her own life to save them.

I loved my story. It made me feel good about being so brave. I was sure that if I ever had the opportunity, I would certainly end up with many friends who would be forever grateful for my help.

As I walked along the trail after Mother, I knew that if a coyote ever did make an appearance, I would be terrified. I would likely even forget to curl, point and prepare my tail, let alone rush to the defense of the other forest creatures.

Still, I could dream, couldn't I? I could pretend that I was brave and fearless. Maybe one day I would get to do something heroic. I needed to be ready. I was sure that it would take something quite spectacular to win myself a friend.

By the time I had finished my daydream, Mother was

slipping under a wooden fence and heading straight for a garden filled with all manner of good things. I put aside my dreams and plunged right in. Never had I seen so much good eating.

We feasted all the rest of the night. Toward morning I nudged up against Mother, mindful of her quills, and said sleepily, "I'm full. Is it time to go home now?"

Mother looked at me and laughed softly. "My, you certainly are full. Just look at you. You can hardly walk."

I looked down at myself. My sides were bulging. I really had overeaten but it had all been so good.

"Well, I guess I'd better get you home while you can still make your way through the forest," Mother said. "Come along then."

I followed Mother. I had seen only one lone rabbit down at the far end of the garden and I made no attempt to get acquainted. Now as we started down the path I was glad that my dream was not coming true. I was glad that the path ahead of us was not filled with chattering squirrels and rabbits and skunks and woodchucks. I was glad that I would not need to be rushing at coyotes and driving them back with the quills in my tail. I was much too full and much too sleepy to be rushing anywhere. I feared that I might never make it home. I just wanted to flop right down where I was and have myself an all-day sleep.

But Mother kept prodding me. "Come on, dear. We must get home before the sun comes up," she reminded me.

I walked along behind her, not paying much attention to the dangers of the forest. Not paying much attention to anything.

Somewhere overhead morning birds were beginning to stir in the branches. "It must already be past our bedtime," I mumbled to myself and yawned sleepily.

"Come along, dear," Mother said again and I did try to hasten my steps.

We were almost home and I was thinking about how nice it would be to climb up into my tree and perch drowsily against a couple branches - that is, if I could make it up the tree. I had never felt so full or so heavy in my entire life. I wasn't even sure that I could climb. For the first time in ages I envied the rabbits who had their homes on the ground.

"We're almost there," Mother said with satisfaction. "It's just beyond . . . Oh, my!"

Mother's sharp intake of breath and quick exclamation brought my head up quickly.

There in the path, directly in front of us, was the largest animal that I had ever seen in my entire life. His sharp, beady eyes were fastened upon us, his mouth was slightly open exposing a row of white, wicked-looking teeth. As I looked, his tongue whipped out and swished the drool from his lips.

"A coyote," I heard Mother exclaim. "Quick."

The animal was moving toward us. I didn't have to ask Mother what he intended to do.

"Curl," Mother flung at me before she tightened herself into a round ball of pointed prickles.

I was so frightened that I could not think straight. What was it I was to do? I couldn't remember. I couldn't think. I could only shake.

The big animal moved toward Mother. He reached

out his long pointed nose. I could see Mother's tail twitch in readiness but just before she was given an opportunity to slap, the animal pulled back and moved around her directly toward me.

For one awful moment, I froze. The long nose reached out toward me and nudged me gently as though to check me out. I knew that the next thing I would feel would be the long, sharp teeth. My fear drove me into a ball. It was the first correct step. "Now what? Now what?" my dizzy head kept asking.

"Point," my instinct answered. "Point."

At just the right minute my quills were raised. I heard the coyote give a startled little yelp and knew that he had drawn back.

I did not dare open my eyes. I curled up more tightly and pointed my quills outward in every direction.

"What is that third thing?" I asked myself in panic. "Rule three? Rule three?" For what seemed like a very long minute I could not remember. I felt the coyote reach out toward me again.

Then it came to me. "Prepare the tail to strike."

I readied my tail, hoping with all of my heart that I wouldn't be called upon to use it.

I felt something close to me again. I was sure that I would feel the sharp teeth soon. I waited. I knew the nose was very close to me now. I still waited, trembling. I felt a movement very near to my body. I was sure that I could feel the hot breath of the coyote on the back of my neck. I gathered my strength together and swung my tail with all of the energy that I could muster.

I wasn't prepared for the result. I knew that I had struck something - hard. In my blindness I wasn't sure what I had hit. That is, until I heard the coyote. With a sharp cry of pain he jumped back from me. He yelped again and began to dance and stamp about. I still didn't dare to look. With a whine of pain and anger he started off down the trail at a gallop. I could hear him crying long after he had left us on the trail.

I lay there trembling. Wondering when he would return to seek his revenge. I don't know if I ever would have dared to uncurl had not Mother spoken to me.

"Good work, Pordy." she said. "You did well. He must have had a dozen quills buried in his nose. He won't be fooling with another porcupine, you can be sure of that."

I still did not relax. I just lay there shaking and trembling.

"You can come out now, Pordy. It's quite safe," Mother prompted.

I took a deep breath - but I did not uncurl.

"Pordy. Pordy, we must get home. It's late," said Mother.

Slowly I began to relax my quills and even dared to uncurl just a bit. One by one I opened my eyes to squint at the day. Already the sun was climbing into the sky. I knew that we belonged up in one of the nearby trees.

"Let's go," said Mother.

I uncurled then and when Mother moved forward I managed to follow her. I was still so shaky that I could hardly walk. I was sure that I'd never manage to climb. But when we reached our tree I was able to climb up the trunk, right behind Mother.

"You did very well, dear," Mother told me again as we settled in among the branches. "I couldn't have done better myself.''

I began to feel pretty smug about it all. I had done quite well. I had sure sent that coyote on its way. Why, if I ever had a chance to protect the young creatures of the forest, I was sure that I'd do just fine.

Even as the thought came to me, I quickly dismissed it. Meeting that coyote had been the scariest thing that had ever happened to me. I was not about to wish for that again - not even for the opportunity to be a heroine. Not in a million years. No, I would need to think of another way to make friends with the forest young. Fighting off a pack of coyotes was too risky a business. I shuddered and closed my eyes. I was thankful to still be all in one piece.

# Chapter Thirteen

## *The Storm*

I wasn't eager to head back to the garden again. Occasionally I recalled the delicious food. My mouth watered and I smacked my lips and drooled. But I also remembered the encounter with the coyote and the hair on the back of my neck tightened and my quills threatened to raise. It was all I could do to keep from curling up in a tight ball.

It didn't appear to have concerned Mother. She often talked about going back to the garden. I knew that it wouldn't be long before we'd be making the trip again but I certainly didn't encourage it by being anxious to go.

My daydream had changed. Instead of being on the ground and fighting off the threatening coyotes, I now saw myself safely in the branches of the tallest tree in our part of the forest.

In my dream, the young forest creatures had all gathered for an evening of games. I watched from up high - not only because I liked to watch their game - but also because I knew that in their excitement they had forgotten to post a sentry.

The game continued with the playing youngsters oblivious to the fact that no one had been posted to watch for danger. But I knew. Up in my tree I was on guard on their behalf. I looked this way and that, peering down through the leaves of the tree branches, studying the gathering shadows as the evening sun sank lower and lower in the western sky.

What was that? Did something move just beyond the hazelnut bushes? The young players were all much too preoccupied to notice. Was something creeping through the tall grasses by the cluster of willows?

Yes. Yes, it was a bear. No, two bears. No, a great big bear and her two half-grown cubs. Mother had told me that mother bears with cubs were the most dangerous. There were three hungry bears. They were looking for a young rabbit or groundhog or maybe a squirrel. I saw them from my spot up in the branches.

They were getting closer and closer to the players. The game went on with chattering, laughing, teasing and name-calling. No one had noticed the creeping bears. No one, that is, except me way up in the tree.

As the biggest bear was about to spring forward and grab Tugsy Rabbit, I pulled myself erect on the limb and screamed with all of the air in my lungs, "Watch out! A bear! Run!"

All the little animals were terrified. As they wheeled around to spot the danger, they also saw me high up in the tree. Of course they didn't wait to say, "Thank you." No, they dashed quickly for cover just out of reach of the hungry - and now angry - bears.

Just in time. The big bear's paw just brushed the tail of Tugsy as he whisked away down the bunny burrow.

As soon as I saw that everyone was safely tucked into their own hiding places, I called down to the bear family, "Go away. Leave our woods. You can't hunt here."

The bears were angry. But what could they do? I was way up in the branches of the tree, high above their heads. All they could do was growl angrily and then slowly leave as I had ordered them to do. After all, there was little use trying to hunt for young animals in a section of the woods where such an alert sentry was always on duty. They decided to take their hungry stomachs and go elsewhere.

It would be some time before the frightened little animals dared to stick their noses out of the safety of their homes again. When they did venture forth, you would not have believed the clamor. They were all so excited and so thankful. They were eager to make friends with the little porcupine up in the tree who had saved them from certain capture.

They called to me, thanked me and requested that I come down and join their game. All of them wanted me for their friend. They promised that they would never again forget to post a sentry. They would never be caught off-guard again. Why, just think what could have happened had I not been such a good and faithful friend, alert on their behalf.

I would be very modest about it all. I would say it was really nothing much, that I had been glad to watch out for them. I might remind them that I had nothing else to do with my time anyway.

They would insist that I join in their play. They would assure me that I wasn't too slow or too ugly or any of those other things that I knew myself to be. It was a wonderful daydream.

I never shared the dream with Mother. Would she understand how important it was to me to have a friend? I was certain that the only way to earn my way into good standing with the other forest young was to find a way to be heroic.

So every night when they played their games, I watched from my position up in the tree. I never did see them forget to post a sentry - but I was quite willing to wait for them to forget - and I wanted to be ready.

Mother seemed to be getting more and more restless.

"Perhaps we should try the orchard again," she said one day, surprising me with her words.

Immediately I thought of my dream to save the forest young by protecting them from the bears due to my warning. I didn't want to miss a chance to fulfill that dream. Would Mother understand if I tried to explain it to her?

"What if bears come?" I began in a faltering voice.

Mother misunderstood my question entirely.

"What about the bears, Pordy?" she said casually. "We would be almost as safe on the ground as in the tree. Black bears can climb too, you know."

I hadn't known that. I began to tremble. Here I had thought I was safe in the tree. I had been dreaming of being the sentry from my hidden place of safety among the branches and now Mother was telling me that bears could climb. "Even mother bears with cubs," I reasoned. "And they are the most dangerous."

"It is easier to curl tightly and point our quills on the ground than it is in the tree," Mother went on, making my whole body shudder. Now I had a new fear to cope with. I guess I wouldn't have a chance to be a sentry after all.

Then an old fear washed over me, making me shake again.

"But the trap . . ." I began.

"Yes, we would need to watch out for traps," Mother agreed. She never even stopped chewing. It seemed a little thing to her.

"Or maybe we should go back to the garden," she mused. "I'm sure the vegetables are even better by now."

I wasn't sure which fate was the most frightening - the orchard with its traps - or the garden with the coyotes on the path. The thought of either one had me quivering.

"Well, it's too late to go tonight," Mother said and I breathed a sigh of relief, "but perhaps we should make the trip as soon as the moon is up tomorrow."

I shivered. Once Mother had made up her mind, she'd go and I knew that I wouldn't stay alone while she went.

We finished our feeding and prepared for a day's rest. I dreaded the thought of the coming evening. Mother would be off - either north to the garden or east to the orchard. Either direction seemed to be filled with peril.

Late in the afternoon I was awakened. At first I couldn't figure out what had roused me. Then I realized that our tree was doing a lot more weaving back and forth than was normal.

Mother stirred restlessly in her sleep and switched her position closer to the tree trunk.

"Mother!" I called up to her. She stirred again but

did not waken.

"Mother!" I called more loudly.

She opened her eyes slightly, then let them close again.

"Mother!" I cried the third time. "The wind is blowing really hard."

Our tree was waving back and forth. I wondered if I'd be able to hold on. Even with my long claws, I feared that I'd lose my grip.

Mother stirred. She looked surprised as her glance traveled up the tree trunk to where the tips of the branches whipped back and forth above our heads.

"The wind is blowing," I said in explanation.

She nodded. Then she moved cautiously, careful not to lose her footing on the branch.

"A storm," she stated. "Looks like a storm is moving in."

I looked above me. How dark the sky was above our heads. Heavy clouds scuttled over the treetops, seeming so close to the uppermost branches that I wondered if they might get caught in them. The clouds were dark and menacing, not white and fluffy, and they moved quickly as though in a tremendous hurry to get somewhere.

"It's going to rain," I whimpered. I hated the rain.

"Yes," agreed Mother. "I fear it is."

"We can't go to the orchard tonight," I hurried on. At least that was one thing in the storm's favor.

"No," said Mother. "Not tonight."

"And we can't go to the garden either," I continued quickly.

"No," replied Mother. "Not to the garden either."

She sounded sad about it.

"We'll just have to stay here," I said to confirm the fact.

A sudden, strong gust of wind had me clinging to the branch for dear life. Mother answered me but her words were whipped away on the wind. I could not hear her reply. We both clung to the tree, trying desperately to keep from being blown right out of its branches.

When the wind quieted some, Mother spoke again.

"We may have to take shelter on the ground," she said.

I thought of all my recent daydreams. I had convinced myself that our woods were full of coyotes and bears and other dreadful creatures. Creatures that were out to catch any small, unsuspecting animal. I did not wish to be on the ground. Even a tree, whipped by the wind, seemed safer to me than the ground with the terrible hunters.

"I'd rather stay here," I said with a shudder.

"The wind often takes trees down when it blows this hard," Mother informed me.

I hadn't known that. I had assumed that nothing, absolutely nothing, could fell one of our big trees.

I was about to argue with Mother when another strong gust of wind brought a big tree across the glade from us crashing to the ground. I watched in horror as it fell, taking smaller trees along with it, splintering and tearing and falling with a loud crash. Huge roots were laid bare, tearing up a whole section of forest undergrowth and grasses, and exposing a large, jagged hole in the forest floor.

I could not believe my eyes. Surely the wind was not

a stronger force than the trees.

At the very instant I argued in thought, another tree, even closer to us, blew down in the storm.

"We need to get on the ground and under cover." said Mother. "Our tree might go down."

"But . . ." I cried into the fierce wind. With the trees uprooting large sections of the forest floor, it didn't appear that one was safe on the ground either.

Then the rain started. It came in torrents, driven by the merciless wind, whipping at our coats, pulling at our bodies, splashing into our faces.

"We'd better go," said Mother. "It will be much harder to hold on now."

I still wanted to argue but I followed Mother down the tree trunk, backing slowly, carefully, clinging to the wet bark with all four of my clawed feet. It was hard making the descent. The bark was slippery from the slashing rain and the wind kept tearing at our long fur.

We were more than halfway down when a strong gust of wind tore at our home. I could hear the tearing and groaning as the roots began to pull free from the soil. The tree shivered, then heaved and I knew that we were going down.

"Hang on," shouted Mother above the whine of the wind.

I hung on. With all of my strength I dug in my claws and held on.

It was a strange sensation. From being right-side-up, I went to being on a slant. The tree began to turn as it fell and I was first on top of the trunk, then on the underside, then on top again. I was feeling dizzy. Suddenly the tree seemed to pitch forward and I was

wrong-side-up and falling fast. But I was still hanging on. My four claws were all tightly imbedded in the trunk of the tree, that is, until there was a dull, loud plunk and I felt myself thrown through the air as the tree settled in against the earth with a giant groan.

When I landed, the force of my fall knocked all of the air out of my lungs. I lay there blinking, fighting hard to breathe again. I didn't know where I was or how I got there, but I did know that I wasn't where I was meant to be.

It was some minutes before I could catch my breath and sort out what had happened. Before I could think clearly again.

I was on my back looking up at a sky filled with angry clouds and wildly whipping treetops. Cold, miserable rain was pelting directly into my face. Tree branches and leaves seemed all around me, almost smothering me with their closeness.

I wasn't sure if I was hurt or not. I felt that I surely must be and, for a moment, I was afraid to move. The position of being on my back was uncomfortable and, instinctively, I struggled to right myself.

Soon I discovered that one hind foot sent a strange pain shooting through my body when I tried to move it, but I was thankful to discover that I was not pinned by any of the branches. I could move even though the effort brought a groan to my lips.

But I was okay. I had survived the fall. I was okay.

Then I thought of Mother. Where was Mother? Was she all right? Had she been hurt? How would I find her in all the mess and confusion?

"Mother," I called, trying to shout above the noise

of the storm. "Mother, where are you?"

Off to my left, I heard a slight stirring. For one moment, panic seized me. What if it was a coyote or a fox or a bear - just waiting for me to make my presence known? Were they poised ready to pounce? I pressed my body back among the broken branches and held my breath.

"Pordy? Pordy, are you okay?" It was Mother's voice. I threw away all caution and struggled free of the tree's broken limbs.

"I'm here, Mother," I cried. "Right here."

Through the rain and wind I could see the outline of my Mother as she made her way slowly toward me. She was limping slightly but she seemed to be all right. I hurried to meet her, pressing my nose up against her and telling her how glad I was to see her.

"We must get in out of the storm," she said. "There is a rock outcropping over by the pasture fence. I think we should go there. It isn't safe here in the forest with so many trees going down."

I agreed. I followed Mother as she led the way through the rain.

We pushed our bodies under the rocky ledge and tried to quiet our shaking. It had been a frightening ordeal. To lose one's home and be forced out into the driving rain to find cover among the rocks was not a pleasant experience. Both of us were limping, having taken quite a nasty fall. We had not eaten. And both of us knew that we'd not venture forth to feed in the storm.

We snuggled together, mindful of one another's quills, and tried to warm the shivers of cold and fear from our bodies. It was almost morning before we stopped trembling.

By morning the storm had blown itself out. Rain was still falling but the wind had died down.

"I think the storm will soon pass," Mother whispered to me.

"What do we do now?" I asked her.

"Oh, there are lots of trees still standing," she said with little concern. "We just need to find a new home."

"But that was *our* tree," I answered quickly. "That was where the forest young always came to play their games. How can I be sentry if . . ." I stopped short. Mother knew nothing about my daydreams of rescuing my forest friends. Well, not my friends, really. Not yet. But they would be once . . .

I hung my head. It seemed that now there was no way for me to ever be a heroine. There was no way at all that I could break down the barriers and be admitted into the close circle of forest friendships. I would always, always be alone.

# Chapter Fourteen

# *Friendship*

All of the forest creatures had been affected by the storm. Like Mother and I, most of them had hidden away somewhere in the forest while the storm was at its worst. As soon as they were sure that the storm had moved on, heads began to peek out and little creatures came from hollow logs, underground burrows, under rocky ledges or some other secret place.

Our forest home was an awful mess. Homes had been swept away by the wind, flooded by the rain or torn away by uprooted trees. The animals gathered in silent clusters, surveying the damage to our world.

Mother and I hung back. We had never taken a role of leadership in our little community. Indeed, we had never seen ourselves as friends of the other animals. I had hoped that would change, but now it seemed that our whole world was upside down. I blinked away tears of disappointment and told myself that my silly secret dreams would never come true. I would never do anything heroic and I would most certainly never have a friend.

Mother and I didn't feel up to climbing a new tree right away. I still walked with a limp because my left hind leg had been hurt in my fall. Mother had an ugly cut on her right front paw. We wanted to heal a bit before taking to the upper limbs of the trees again. Besides, we were still somewhat nervous about heights. Every time a little breeze began to flutter the leaves above our heads, I would start feeling panicky again.

At first the other animals seemed to be skittish, too. It didn't take much of a noise to send the rabbits dodging into underground burrows or squirrels scampering up the trees. After a few days things began to get back to normal again.

Mother and I had not left our rocky overhang except to do some feeding at night. I didn't feel safe on the ground, but I didn't like the thought of climbing way up against the sky again, either.

I felt sad that the home base for all the forest games had fallen in the storm. But the little animals were creative. Soon they had picked another tree as home base and were playing their evening games again.

I could no longer pretend to be sentry. From my position under the rock ledge, I couldn't see much of anything.

Gradually my leg was feeling much better and Mother's foot was also healing quickly. She hadn't begun to talk about the orchard or the garden again, but I feared that the idea would soon come to her. Before long she was walking without a limp and my leg was almost as good as new.

"I think . . ." she began one night and I was sure that she was going to suggest traveling either north or east. I wasn't sure which one made me tremble the most.

"I think," Mother said again, "that it is time for us to pick another tree."

I expelled the air I had been holding. Finding a new home sounded much better to me than heading toward the orchard with its traps or the garden path with its coyotes.

"I think so, too," I seconded.

"Where would you like to live?" continued Mother. "Would you like to be over beside the stream or across the meadow or maybe on the far side of the hill?"

I had never thought of moving away before.

"Why don't we just stay here?" I asked Mother.

"Well, there's no reason for us to stay. Our home is gone. We don't have any family - or friends."

It was true but it made me feel sad anyway. I wanted friends.

"Well, we sort of have friends," I said to Mother.

She looked surprised. "Have you met some of the little creatures, dear?" she asked.

"No. No, but I . . . I know the names of . . . of some of the . . . the little animals," I maintained.

"You should get to know them, dear," said Mother and I knew that she still didn't understand. They would not want me for a friend. Not unless I did something really spectacular to earn their friendship. It was looking more and more like I'd never be able to do that.

"Well, let's go see if we can find a nice tree in the area, then," Mother interrupted my thinking.

I followed along after her, my head held low. My thoughts were still heavy with the knowledge that I did not have a friend. Not a single one.

I wasn't paying attention to where I was going or what I was doing. I was feeling much too sad. Why, I could have walked right into a coyote or a bear - I was that careless. But I didn't. I almost walked into a small wood mouse instead.

"Watch out," I heard a little voice cry, and my head came up quickly.

There she was. It was the same little mouse that I had met on the trail before.

"You almost stepped on my thistle. I'm . . . I'm taking it home . . . for the seed. It's very good to eat, you know," she said, her voice squeaky-high with her nervousness.

"I . . . I'm sorry. I didn't mean . . . I wasn't paying attention. I . . . I'm sorry," I stammered.

She seemed to relax then. She even managed a wobbly smile. "That's all right. Sometimes I don't watch where I'm going either," she said. Then she giggled.

I started to relax a bit, too. "I'm really sorry," I said again. "I was so deep in thought I . . . Could I . . . could I help you? I'll . . . I'll be happy to carry it home for you. It looks heavy for . . . for such a . . . a small mouse."

I stopped and flushed. It surprised me that I had said so much. She looked so tiny and the thistle looked so big. All of my talking might just scare her more. Yet, she hadn't run away. I was afraid that she would. I didn't want her to go but I didn't know what to do or say to keep her here.

She shook her head. She didn't seem to be trembling quite as much when she spoke again. "I'll manage. I'm used to carrying food home." She smiled shyly again. "Sometimes it's hard to remember where home is since the storm. We've already moved three times.

Mother had to find just the right spot . . . where she feels safe again.''

"I . . . I'm sorry," I said and my voice was only a whisper.

She sighed deeply, then looked at me sadly.

"Did , . . did your home get destroyed in the storm, too?'' she asked, her little eyes wide with the seriousness of the question.

I nodded my head.

"Yours?" I asked her.

"We were flooded out," she said slowly, and looked very sad.

"I'm sorry," I managed to say again, swallowing hard.

"And you?" she prompted.

"Our . . . our tree was blown right over," I said, my eyes getting big as I thought of the scary trip to the ground.

"Were you up in it?" she asked. It was her turn to look frightened at the thought.

I nodded.

"It must have been awful," she sympathized

"It . . . it was," I blurted. "I . . . I hurt my foot in the fall and Mother had a cut on her front paw. We had to hide under the rocks for days while we healed. We are just now going to look for a new home."

I bit my tongue. My, I had been prattling on. She would be quite upset with me.

But she didn't seem to be. She had not moved away from me. Not even an inch. She stood right where she was just as though . . . just as though we were friends.

"Did . . . did you find a new home yet?" I dared to

ask her.

She nodded and pointed to a clump of willows on the edge of the meadow. "We are over there now," she said.

"That's . . . that's quite close," I said and I was pleased.

"Where . . . where are you going to live?" she asked me.

"Mother did talk about going over by the stream or across the meadow or over the hill but I . . . I didn't want to . . . to move away from my friends," I said.

She looked at me and nodded. I decided that I had to explain myself. To tell the real truth.

"Well, really," I said, my head lowering, "really - I don't have any friends - not really. That is - not yet. I would like a friend but so far . . ."

"Why?" she asked simply.

"Why, what?" I responded, not understanding her question.

"Why don't you have friends?"

"Well . . . well, because . . . because . . . well, no one wants a . . . a porcupine for a friend. I mean . . ."

"Nonsense! You are really very nice. Mother says that porcupines are always very nice - and polite - and thoughtful. And Granny says that porcupines never cause any trouble with the other animals as long as one leaves them properly alone."

"But I don't want to be left alone," I cut in quickly. "I . . . I'd like a . . . a friend to . . ."

"I would be happy to have you for a friend," said the little wood mouse without a moment's hesitation.

"You would?" I could not keep the tremor from my

voice.

"Of course."

"But I . . . I mean, I don't even know how to . . . to *be* a friend," I admitted.

She giggled again. "You are being a friend now," she said with a little shrug.

"But I . . ." I hadn't done anything. That is, I hadn't done anything spectacular.

"To *have* a friend you must *be one*," said the little mouse. "That is what Granny always says. You . . . just . . . just be a friend. You care about other folks. That's all you do to be a friend."

"Oh, I care," I was quick to say. "I really do. I mean, I . . . I . . ." I didn't want to share with her just how much I cared. Or tell her about my daydreams of how I would take care of the forest creatures.

"So - you *are* a friend," she said as she looked right at me and gave me a little smile. "You can start by being my friend. And . . . and I will introduce you to some of the others - if you are interested."

"Oh, I am. I am," I said quickly.

"Pordy?" It was Mother calling. She had traveled on ahead and when she realized that I was not following close behind her, she had come looking for me.

"Here," I answered. "I'm here."

"Do you have to go?" asked the little mouse.

"I . . . I . . . yes, I suppose so. Mother must be worried about me. But wait. Don't . . . don't go away. I . . . I think she's coming. She'll . . . she'll want to . . . to meet you," I said quickly.

I could hardly wait to share my good news with Mother. Why, this was even better than any of my dreams.

"Mother, this is my new friend," I said excitedly as soon as Mother came back along the trail.

"I'm Skippy," said my new friend to Mother.

Mother stopped and looked at me and then at Skippy. A smile began to lighten her face.

"I'm pleased to meet you, Skippy," she said to the little mouse. "So you have met Pordillia. She has been wishing for a friend."

Skippy looked from Mother back to me and smiled a little smile again. "One never has too many friends," she said lightly. "That's what Granny always says."

Mother nodded her head. Her eyes were shining. "You have a very wise Granny," she said to the little mouse.

"I know," said Skippy. "She knows that friends are special just because . . . just because they are friends."

I looked at Skippy and nodded in understanding. I had never felt happier in my whole life. I wasn't a heroine. I hadn't done one thing that was special. It had all happened so simply, so ordinarily, so . . . so naturally. I had met someone, had offered friendship, and now I had a friend. A real friend. I couldn't help but grin as I looked at Skippy. It was going to be so nice to have a friend of my own.